MW00884726

Book 1: My Cousin, the Piney
Written by Tony DiGerolamo

First Edition: September 2019
Published in Laurel Springs, NJ by
South Jersey Rebellion Productions

Library of Congress Reference Number: TXu2-107-267
Version 1.3
Print: **ISBN:** 9781673137736
ebook: **ASIN:** B07XVCWVCK

Cover Art by Vig Starmax (visit www.thewebcomicfactory.com for more)

The Pineys™ is a trademark of Anthony M. DiGerolamo

Special thanks to: Marilyn DiGerolamo and Christian Beranek

Visit the Galloway Hunting Lodge website at www.gallowayhuntinglodge.com

Welcome to the Hunt!
Tony W.
3/1/24

Contents

Prologue: 1732

Leeds Point was just a dot on the map in the Province of West Jersey, barely a blip on the radar of King George II. Long before muskets were raised in revolution against George III, the people of Leeds Point eeked out a living farming in the sandy woods of the Pine Barrens. It was isolated. The only news of the outside world came to this wooded area via stagecoach, and most that heard it didn't care.

Mother Leeds was one of the villagers. Trapped in her life raising 12 children, for which she knew there was never enough food, money, or supplies, she struggled more than most. She wanted all her progeny to live at first, but when she became pregnant for the 13th time, it was too much.

Something snapped in this frail woman, who was already on the brink. In her ragged, sleep-deprived state, she called upon all the forces of Darkness and Satan Himself. "Curse this child!" she screamed. "Let the Devil take it!" And thus was born the Jersey Devil: the monster that has haunted South Jersey and the Pine Barrens ever since.

Or, so the story goes.

The truth was colonial villagers didn't just call up Satan out of the blue. Mother Leeds was a witch. And she didn't just call up a devil; she opened the portals to Hell, allowing hundreds of devils to flood into the Pine Barrens of South Jersey.

But this supernatural phenomenon did not go unnoticed by the nearby villagers of Abe's Hat. A group of hunters banded together to form a secret society to hunt down the devils, send them back to the Darkness and close the portals forever.

This is the story of a group of cousins, cursed by their ancestors, brought together by destiny, and trying to keep South Jersey from going to Hell.

Chapter 1

Lewis Cognata thought himself as a smooth operator. In a casino poker room, he imagined himself as George Clooney in Ocean's 11, but in reality, he came off more like George Castanza in Seinfeld. George Clooney's character probably would've never decided to get off the Atlantic City Expressway to duck the tolls, but when you were a not-so-winning professional poker player, you had to cut corners somewhere.

"Where are you, Lewis?" said Pete in a demanding tone over the headset. "You're into me for eight large, and I do not like to be kept waiting."

"Relax," said Lewis looking for a gas station. "I just got off the Expressway. I'll be back on in a minute."

"You friggin' idiot! There's a stop on the Expressway!"

"I am on fumes, Pete! You want me to break down and have the troopers find me? How long do you think it'll take me to get there by **bus**?!"

"You're a friggin' idiot, ya know that? There's nuthin' off the Expressway but empty plazas and out of work hillbillies!"

"Hillbillies? What am I? In Alabama?"

"Pineys, dumbass! New Jersey's version of hillbillies!"

"Seriously?"

"Yeah, seriously!"

"Well, they gotta have cars and gas, right?"

"Yeah, and banjos and inbred cousins! You miss this tournament; ya better hope one of those backwood gavones gives you an eight grand tip after he butt rapes you senseless!"

Lewis grimaced to himself as Pete hung up. The gambler was driving his dark green jeep, which he had meticulously kept in working order since he bought it new twelve years ago. Unfortunately, it was starting to show its age. The top had faded somewhat, although the snaps still held together well. He worried that if he ever removed the top again for the summer, he'd tear the whole thing stretching it back on. Lewis needed a new car and a win.

He'd bet, both figuratively and literally, everything on this professional poker thing. The gambler sensed it wasn't working, but there was no backing out now. His savings were way too shallow;

4

there was no way he could get his job back at the carpet store. Pete was unlikely to give him an extension on his loan.

Lewis was a fit, handsome guy in that South Jersey Italian way. He had a thick mop of black hair, perfectly groomed about his round, pudgy face, an open $330 collared shirt with a 40 dollar gold chain, black slacks, and comfortable black Florsheims. The shirt was open, blowing in the breeze along with his chest hair. He didn't want to sweat himself up before getting into the casino. Lewis probably could've walked into most casinos and started dealing Blackjack like he belonged there. He dressed like a dealer and probably could run three or four hands before a pit boss would notice.

At the corner of trees and the middle of fucking nowhere, Lewis spotted a scattering of farm-y buildings and something called "Abe Hat's General Store." He had driven into the middle of a sort of town out in the Pine Barrens. There was a stoplight, which was probably the busiest intersection in town. It had signs nearby for yard sales, church suppers, and a high school talent show.

"Jesus," muttered Lewis to himself. "Could this place be any more cornball? I'd shoot myself if I lived here!"
The engine of the jeep coughed and sputtered. He wasn't out of gas yet, but he figured he had less than a mile.

Cursing his own stupidity, he pulled up to the store where two Pineys were sitting on the steps. Lewis thought it looked like something out of a Norman Rockwell painting. There was some fat, gray-haired guy in a hunter's outfit playing the harmonica and his buddy, also dressed in hunters' flannel, playing a banjo. The gray-haired guy had glasses, a soul patch, and a nervous kind of energy that probably belonged to a guy half his age. His buddy was tall, lanky, dark hair, more laid back with a wooden coffee stirrer hanging out of his mouth. He was a handsome guy, probably in his early 40s, although he appeared younger. They both looked like they spent their days on top of a tractor or talking about how the weather would be "fixin'" to mess with the crops.

"Christ, I gotta deal with these yokels," muttered Lewis, cutting the engine. "Probably taking a break from having sex with their cousins."

The gray-haired man, who had a red baseball cap proclaiming "Piney Power," eyed him warily. Lewis put on the charm.

"Hey, fellas, sorry to interrupt," he began. "I'm running on fumes. You gotta gas station nearby? I mean, **really** nearby?"

"Highway's the closet place," said the one with the banjo and a hunter's cap.

"You should download that gas app to be sure," added harmonica, pulling out his smartphone. "It's like Gas-up or something."

"You guys are some hi-tech hillbillies," joked Lewis.

"Pineys," corrected harmonica, pointing to his hat and frowning.

"Uh, yeah," said Lewis changing gears. "The store open? I need some gum."

"Sure, go inside," invited harmonica.

Lewis got a weird vibe from the Pineys, like they were sizing him up. When he reached the doorway of the store, he noticed a line of white powder across the opening.

"Somebody spill something?" said Lewis curiously.

"Why? That bother you? Go inside," insisted banjo.

The Pineys seemed to tense up. Lewis didn't get it.

"Fine," said Lewis cautiously.

Lewis stepped across the threshold, and the two men seemed to relax.

"Gum's on the counter," said harmonica. "Let me know if you need change."

"You run the store?"

"Yeah," said harmonica impatiently.

"Then why don't you come in and ring up my purchase? I'm a customer."

"Because I'm **busy**," replied harmonica, increasingly annoyed.

Lewis went to the counter and helped himself to some gum. He bought an even three dollars' worth and left the bills on the counter.

It was about then that a disheveled black kid in a denim jacket, maybe 19, stumbled out of the woods across the street. He limped toward the general store. Lewis was downloading the Gas app and noticed the Pineys watching the kid. He came out of the store with his gum in hand.

"You, uh, really need to get out of here," warned banjo.

The kid made it to the store's doorway but stopped as the one with the banjo said, "You sure you want to go in there?"

The kid looked down at the line of white powder and then suddenly started walking away.

"You're not welcomed here," assured harmonica.

"Jesus!" thought Lewis. "One wrong turn into the woods and New Jersey really turns into the South in the '50s. Were these guys for real?!"

The kid, dazed from maybe lack of water, turned around and stumbled back onto the asphalt. He headed down the middle of the right lane. Banjo and harmonica began to stand up. Banjo flicked away his coffee stirrer.

"No-no-no," said Lewis. "You're not really doing this, right? This is not 1950!"

Harmonic pulled a piece of tubing out of his jacket pocket.

"Here, go siphon some gas and get lost. This ain't your business."

"You had that tubing ready?"

"I'm always ready," assured harmonica.

The kid continued up the street, unsteady. Harmonica drew a revolver and let it hang by his side. Banjo strapped the banjo to his back and pulled out what looked like two little swords. They started to flank the helpless kid. Lewis thought about getting in his car and driving. He liked to think of himself as a little bit gangsta, but deep down, he had heart. He knew instantly he could never live with himself if he let these two redneck maniacs cut this kid down.

The kid abruptly stopped, and Lewis ran around the gray-haired fat guy, putting himself in between.

"Look, guys, you can't do this!" Lewis pleaded. "This is the 21st century! You'll go to prison for the rest of your lives!"

"Get away from him," insisted Harmonica.

"He doesn't know, Hem," said Banjo.

Lewis had read somewhere that humanizing yourself during a hostage situation made it less likely the hostage-takers would kill you. He jumped on the name.

"Hem? It's Hem. I'm Lewis. And you are?"

"Milton," said Banjo, realizing the tactic. "And he's not gonna talk."

"Kid, what's your name?" asked Lewis.

The kid seemed out of it. He kept looking at the ground and looking forward, wondering what to do.

"He's mentally ill or somethin'," concluded Lewis.

"He's not mentally ill," said Hem impatiently. "When they built the road here, they cut the cemetery in half. They moved the bodies, but it's still consecrated ground."

"So?" said Lewis, not understanding.

"He can't walk across it. It'll burn him," explained Milton.

"Look, I got a banana bread baking back at the store, and I swear ta Christ, if I burn it, Mil...."

"Hem, you're worried about your banana bread?"

"I spent 40 minutes mixing the ingredients!"

"You can **buy** banana bread."

"Oh! You're gonna eat store-bought banana bread when we have fresh bananas?! That's **sick**!"

While the two men bickered, Lewis took the opportunity to try and get the kid out of harm's way.

"Kid! Let's try to run! I'll call the cops, c'mon!"

Lewis pulled the kid a few steps forward, but instantly the asphalt started to burn his shoes. Lewis was fine, but it looked like the kid had stepped onto a giant, hot frying pan. He fell to his knees and hands, which also burned.

"What's wrong? What's wrong?!" demanded Lewis impotently.

"Okay, homemade is better than store-bought. I will concede that point."

"**Thank** you."

The kid was screaming in agony. Lewis looked around, wondering why no one was coming out of any of the houses.

"You gotta help him!" insisted Lewis.

"We can't help him," Hem said impatiently.

"Why?"

"Hem, don't --- "

"The guy you're standing next to? He's a **devil spawn**."

Lewis looked back at Hem, incredulous.

"Dude! That is some messed-up racism!"

"What?!"

"Lewis," Milton tried to calmly explain over the screams. "We're not after him because he's black. That's just the form of the person he bit last."

"I can't believe this guy!" cried Hem, completely outraged. "He defends a level 2 Shifter that stole this guy's identity and calls **us** bigots?!"

"He's a person!" insisted Lewis.

"He is not!" insisted Hem. "Look at what's happening! He's pure evil!"

"It's true," sighed Milton. "Just back away, very slowly. As long as it doesn't see any blood…."

At that moment, a crossbow bolt came sailing out of the woods and landed right into Lewis's right arm.

"Ow!"

"Shelly!" Milton scolded in the direction of the woods.

"Sorry!" a woman's voice replied.

"Kid, try to run!" said Lewis, trying to make a break.

Unfortunately, as soon as Lewis tried to get the kid to his feet, the blood started dripping from his arm, which dribbled on the kid, who immediately reacted. His face widened, his teeth grew pointed, and his eyes turned yellow and cat-like.

"What?" gasped Lewis, trying to make sense of it.

The kid, now clearly a devil spawn, bit into Lewis's thigh. He let out a scream.

"You stupid noob!" snapped Hem, moving forward.

Hem grabbed Lewis by the arm and pumped round after round into the demonic kid. The creature let go of Lewis, and he and Hem both stumbled back across the road into the bushes. Milton moved between the beast and the bushes, waiting for the perfect moment to strike. A gorgeous young woman, presumably Shelly, came running out of the woods, winding a crossbow. She was also dressed in a hunting outfit and cap, although it looked a size too big for her frame. Soft auburn locks bounced around her head as she struggled with the crossbow.

"I really need to add a laser scope," said Shelly. "Or get a sword."

The creature made a few test lunges at Milton, who ducked and blocked them with his swords. Hem stood up and reloaded.

"Sorry, cuz, you're just an intern," reminded Milton.

"Yeah, yer lucky to get a weapon. I had to use a bat until I was 16," said Hem a little bitterly.

"What is happening?" said Lewis, a little overwhelmed by the events and the blood loss. "I think I need a hospital."

"No, we can't explain the bite. Just keep pressure on it. We can't let this one go now that it bit you."

"Why?"

As Lewis talked, he realized the creature was answering his question. It morphed into a distorted mirror version of himself.

"Take him out, Milton. Don't mess around," ordered Hem.

"This is a teachable moment for Shelly," assured Milton. "Watch and learn."

Milton charged the faux-Lewis, and it swung out with claws. Milton sidestepped gracefully, came up with the blades, cut off the arms, twirled, and severed the head in one deft move. The creature's pieces fell to the ground.

"Holy shit!" gasped Lewis.

"Don't-don't," insisted Hem. "Don't encourage him."

Milton, pleased with himself, stood up and looked toward Shelly.

"**That** is how you take out a hellspawn."

Suddenly, the headless and armless torso stood up, pushed Milton aside, and made a break for it. It blundered into a parked car setting off the alarm, and Shelly raised her crossbow.

"I'm on it."

"Wait-wait-wait!" insisted Hem.

The bolt sailed past the devil spawn and lodged itself into Lewis's front tire. Hem aimed at the creature as he advanced.

"You two make us look **incredibly** unprofessional."

Hem fired, striking the creature in the left knee. It immediately stumbled and fell down.

"Ha!" said Hem victoriously.

The creature then rolled into the sewer drain and disappeared into the darkness.

"Shit! Shit-shit-shit!" spat Hem, suddenly changing his tune. "You horned devil fuck-nuts!"

Hem fired into the sewer drain angrily, bullets ricocheting off the metal, briefly illuminating the darkness. He knew there'd be no finding the creature now.

"Goddammit! Goddammit!" Hem shouted to no one.

"Calm down, Hem. For God's sake," said Milton, a little embarrassed. "You must've wasted two hundred dollars in ammo."

"We got plenty of silver bullets," insisted Hem.

"Hey, who's that other guy?" asked Shelly.

Hem suddenly remembered Lewis. Lewis was limping his way away from the trio. They immediately rushed over to him.

"Did you lose sight of him?! Did you?" demanded Hem, aiming his pistol at Lewis. "Are you, you?! **Are you?!**"

"Please! I think I need a doctor," said Lewis. "I should've just left! I'm sorry! I didn't know! I didn't know! I'm sorry!"

"Lewis, it's fine. We're not going to hurt you," assured Milton.

Lewis relaxed a little. Milton whipped out a dagger and sliced Lewis in the arm just enough to ensure his blood was red.

"Blood's red. We're good."

"You said you weren't going to hurt me!"

"I didn't think you'd hold still and let me do it."

"I wouldn't have let you do it! You people are nuts!"

Shelly stepped in, attempting to calm the situation.

"Look, I know my cousins look, sound, and act a little crazy, but they actually know what they're doing. We've all been bit, and we've got a first aid kit back at the store."

"Oh, shit! My banana bread!"

Hem went running back towards the General Store. Lewis looked into Shelly's eyes. She reminded him of the Tinder girls that always turned out to be Ukrainian bots and scam artists. Shelly figured, since she shot him, Lewis deserved at least a chance at a date. The smitten gambler decided if he was going to be late for the tournament, at least he might gamble on getting laid.

Chapter 2

Minutes later, Shelly was bandaging Lewis's thigh and arm while Hem tried to cut off the sides of a burnt banana bread loaf. Milton was on his phone looking up information about the sewer system in Abe's Hat.

"The devils can't cross a line of salt. Hem didn't want to fight the thing in the store. Too much damage to the merchandise," explained Milton.

"Ah, so you guys were testing me. You guys were acting so weird, I almost didn't go into the store. What were you gonna do then?"

Milton sorta shrugged and looked at one of his swords.

"You were gonna cut my head off for not buying gum?!"

"Well, not your **head**. Not at first...."

"Why aren't we out there findin' this thing?"

"He ain't gonna come out until nightfall. Gives us about five hours, but we're gonna need the Lodge," said Milton routinely.

"I hope you're happy, Shelly!" snapped Hem. "Not only do we have to go ask for help, not only do we look like **totally** amateurs--- This banana bread is completely dried out!"

"You should've put cranberries in it. Would've been a lot more moist."

"Well, you should learn to **shoot**, Shelly!"

"I can shoot a gun!"

"Not in this stupid state!"

Hem dropped a plate of burnt banana bread slices on the table before everyone, then stormed back into the kitchen to mope.

"Man, that guy's a powder keg," noted Lewis.

"Hemingway takes the Hunt very seriously," explained Milton.

"Hemingway? Wait, is that his last name or his first name?" asked Lewis.

"First name," explained Shelly. "We all have the last name, Galloway."

"Hemingway Galloway, jeez, no wonder he shortened it. That's a mouthful," noted Lewis.

"Shut up!" came the retort from the kitchen.

"And you're Shelly, right? I'm Lewis. Your boyfriend okay with all this?"

"Oh, I don't have a boy--- Oooooh, you're hitting on me."

"Is it working?"

"My family is a little--- "

Out of the corner of her eye, Shelly spotted Milton reaching for a sword.

12

"Milton, no," she scolded. "Sorry, they're all revved up from the Hunt."

"Well, uh, you guys gonna clue me in on this Hunt or what?" asked Lewis.

"Can't," said Shelly finishing the bandage and taking a slice of banana bread.

"It's a secret," said Milton, not looking up from his phone.

Hemingway stepped back into the room, almost on cue.

"Our ancestors cursed us," he began to explain.

"Hem! You're not supposed to tell people!" reminded Shelly.

"You know the Lodge hates when you do," added Milton.

"Screw the Lodge! I'm not running around the woods all night with this dude answering his questions! And he's gonna have a lot of them! Besides, he's already been bit! He might as well know, in case it gets away."

"Why?" said Lewis worried. "What happens if it gets away?"

"Oh, nothing much. Probably just a series of gruesome murders with your face and fingerprints all over them. The last one killed like seven prostitutes in A.C."

"What? That was one of those things?! We gotta find it!"

"See? Now he doesn't even care about the back story."

"Then don't tell it," muttered Milton through his teeth.

Lewis looked at Hemingway, who considered it for a second and then dismissed the idea.

"Ah, I'm gonna tell it. So it's 1732 in Leeds Point, just down the road, and--- You heard of the Jersey Devil, right?" began Hem.

"The hockey team mascot? Sure. It's like that thing that ran around in the woods and--- Shit!" gasped Lewis putting it together. "Was that thing the Jersey Devil?"

"Technically, there's a lot of Jersey Devils, but no. If that was the original, we'd be picking up your pieces off the roadway and burying them out back," assured Hem.

"The old story goes, Mother Leeds had 13 children, and the last one she cursed to be a devil," Milton said.

"Yeah, only, that's not exactly how it happened. Our ancestors were there. Mother Leeds was a witch and opened the portals to Hell, flooding the woods with hellspawn. Our ancestors started a secret society to hunt them down! Our family has been trying to close the portals ever since," explained Hem.

"Devil hunters. A family business for over 250 years," said Shelly proudly.

As Lewis listened, he let his hand drop, and it brushed against an ancient-looking spittoon on the floor near his chair. Suddenly, he got a vision in his mind. The room shifted, and he was looking at the colonial villagers in 1732. He could see that three looked very much like Hemingway, Milton, and Shelly. Lewis was rattled by the vision for a moment but shook the image away and pretended nothing had happened.

"Um, I don't get it," said Lewis, trying to understand. "Why don't you just close the portal to Hell?"

"Because," said Shelly interrupting Hem before he could say.

Hem nodded and gestured for her to continue. Shelly repeated the story like she had memorized the pledge of allegiance in third grade.

"The problem with devils is that they spawn other devils, and each time they spawn, that opens another portal, but each time we send one back to Hell, that closes one. So until we send them **all** back, the portals are basically stuck open."

Hemingway gestured a "thumbs up." Shelly had the story down.

"See? I pay attention," said Shelly proudly.

"Good, now go change Lewis's tire, Eagle Eye," ordered Hemingway.

Shelly muttered in annoyance and reluctantly got up to go change the tire.

"So just you three against all of Hell, huh?" said Lewis skeptically.

"Oh, we're not the only cousins in the hunting lodge," assured Hemingway. "In fact, I think we got time for a drink."

"Now you **want** to go to the Lodge?" said Milton, incredulous.

"Well, we gotta ask them for help anyway," Hem said, resigned to the inevitable.

The Galloway Hunting Lodge was set on the outskirts of Abe's Hat. It had a gravel parking lot that led up to a very large, old, but sturdy-looking barn. A few pickup trucks and an El Camino were parked in a neat row against the right side of the building. A hand-

14

carved sign above the double barn doors proclaimed "Galloway Hunting Lodge, EST 1733". Hemingway had driven the group over in his restored pickup truck, a blue 1966 Chevy C-10. He skidded into the middle of the lot, not worried about who he might block or where he parked.

"Okay, Lewis, do not talk," instructed Hem.

"Good advice, why don't **you** take it?" suggested Milton.

"What?" asked Hem innocently.

"Cuz, let me do the talking, so you don't immediately piss everyone off," said Milton, almost asking.

"Fine," Hem relented.

The inside of the barn had been converted into a large, comfortable, and modern room. There was a roaring fireplace, several sturdy-looking wooden tables and chairs, and the preserved heads and antlers of deer everywhere on the walls. A group of three hunters played cards at one of the tables, while a fourth texted on his phone while sipping out of a mug of beer. The bartender was a balding, bearded hipster type who was wiping down the bar. He briefly stopped wiping when he spotted the cousins, then continued cleaning.

"Hey, cousins," greeted Milton.

"Cuz." "Hey, cuz." "Cuz." Came back the various replies from the room.

"Why is everyone called cuz?" whispered Lewis to Shelly.

"A lot of us are related, and it's short for cousin," she explained.

"Hey Milton," smiled a middle-aged woman in a hunting cap. "Buy me a drink?"

"Maybe later, Joyce," assured Milton.

"Are you banging, Joyce Whitaker? Her husband owns a gun store!" hissed Hemingway, trying to whisper. "And isn't she an actual cousin?"

"First, she told me they were separated," assured Milton. "Second, she's a collateral cousin. Thrice removed."

"How is that going to make him less pissed off you're banging his wife?"

Shelly punched Hem, trying to derail the conversation.

"Focus, cuz. Focus," she added, mildly embarrassed.

"Are you guys all related?" asked Lewis.

"No!" insisted Shelly. "I mean, some of us are. But it's not like my cousins are a bunch of inbred hillbillies."

"You sure about that?" asked Lewis gingerly.

"Hey, Lee," said Milton to the bartender. "My cousins and I would like to see last year's hunting trophies."

Lee, the bartender, looked at Lewis. Hemingway fidgeted, anxious to get on with it.

"That's for lodge members only, Milton," reminded Lee. "Or family."

"He could be family," offered Hem. "Test him."

"How could I be family?" asked Lewis.

"We have a lot of relatives in South Jersey. The Galloways were in America before America," explained Shelly. "You know your family tree well?"

"Not really. I was adopted."

Lee pulled out a swab and a testing kit.

"Here ya go, just need a swab," said Lee handing it to Lewis.

"No way! I don't want to be on a federal database!" objected Lewis.

"I do the testing," explained Lee. "The test will be strictly confidential. Well, within the Lodge anyway."

"Fine," said Lewis, reluctantly swabbing.

Lee took the swab and sealed it into the test tube.

"Can he get in now?" said Hem, growing impatient.

"I haven't done the test yet."

"It's okay," assured Milton. "He was bit."

"And you guys let your quarry get away? Need new glasses, Hem?" teased Lee.

"Don't be a dick, Lee," Hemingway snapped. "Just open the door."

"He's not supposed to see the door, cuz," reminded Lee.

"Oh, my God," said Hemingway in contempt. "Anyone with half a brain can see that this room is only part of this giant barn! He probably already knows where it is!"

"No, I don't," assured Lewis.

"Well, you could've put a bag over his head or something," suggested the bartender.

"It's broad daylight! We'd look like kidnappers! You wanna keep this place a secret or not?!" snapped Hem.

"Easy, Hem," said Milton. "We barely know, Lewis."

"Yeah, and you said the secret password right in front of him," reminded Lee.

"He probably still doesn't know what it is," insisted Milton.

"I don't know what it is," added Lewis.

"When Milton asked for last year's hunting trophies, he was referencing 1732, the year of the curse. That's the password," explained Hem, impatient.

"Well, now you just told him!" Lee said, stunned that he would explain it.

"I'm not gonna wait here all day, Lee! Open the god damned door!" snapped Hem.

Lee reluctantly hit a switch under the bar. The fireplace swung partially open, revealing a secret passage.

"I'm going to mention this at the next Lodge Council meeting, **cuz**," Lee added threateningly.

"Yeah-yeah, you do that," dismissed Hemingway.

The interior of the back room of the barn was a whole lot of the same, except for one major difference, the hunting trophies were all devil heads. Mounted on the wooden beams and barn walls were hideous horned heads. Most had red, twisted faces, some were as black as onyx, but all had yellow or orange cat-like eyes. Their teeth were sharp, and their horns erupted from their skulls in a variety of twisted ways. Each head was mounted on a wooden plaque with a metal plate with an engraving. Some of the older ones, however, had no metal plates and were intricately carved. It looked like the trophy room after someone went on a shooting spree in Dante's Inferno. On the opposite side were several bookshelves of ancient-looking books underneath gray-glass cases.

"Holy shit," muttered Lewis. "What the Hell is this place?"

"The Lodge, dude. Haven't you been paying attention?" explained Hemingway.

Hem pointed toward a massive devil head above a second fireplace. The devil's face looked like it had been pummeled to a pulp, and one of its massive horns was broken off. The inscription on the bottom said, "Hemingway Galloway" and had a date from the '80s.

"What the Hell is that?!" gasped Lewis.

"That's what you call luck," said a surly cousin with a flannel jacket and a beer in one hand.

"Uh, yeah, right, Carl," said Hemingway sarcastically. "I only took it out with a baseball bat while you were still wettin' your daddy's bed!"

"Doesn't even make any sense," muttered Milton, embarrassed for him.

"It doesn't have to make sense when you **kick ass**," assured Hem.

Hemingway jumped up on a chair just to slap the cheek of the devil's head.

"How ya doin', Todd."

"That thing's name is Todd?!" asked Lewis, incredulous. "What level is that?"

"He's Level 25 plus Bone Crusher," assured Hemingway. "Cause anything over 25 gets its own name."

"And you called it Todd?"

"Yeah. I hate that name. Right Todd?"

"Hem…ing…way," hissed Todd's head.

The old hunter, surprised by the words, grabbed the nearest beer mug and smashed it over the devil's face.

"You-wanna-go-again?! You-wanna-go?! You level 25+ piece of shit!" added Hem, punching it several times.

Lewis had another vision. This time the room disappeared, and he was standing in Abe's Hat. A 16-year-old Hemingway smashed a bat over the Devil Todd's head, snapping off his horn while singing a few bars from the Rocky Theme. Lewis returned to the present a few seconds later and staggered backward a step.

"Is th-that th-th-thing alive?!" he asked in a panic.

"Well, technically, devils aren't really alive to begin with," added Shelly.

"But some of the big ones," Milton admitted. "They can't really die. Our ancestors figured out that if you cut off their heads, their bodies go back to Hell headless."

"As long as his head's up here and his headless corpse is stumbling around Hell--- It's not like he's gonna do much," said Hemingway, punching the devil one last time.

18

"That thing must've been--- What? Nine feet?" estimated Lewis.

"Twelve at least," assured Hemingway. "A record-sized devil for the lodge. Plus, I was only 16."

"And he hasn't shut up about it since," muttered another cousin as he sipped his beer.

Hemingway gestured to a mounted devil head with a tire track across its face.

"Oh, sure, listen to Wallace, over there. The guy that had to run over a Level 4 Flesh Eater, his first kill, with a **mini-van**!"

"A kill's a kill," smiled Wallace.

"Well, maybe go gas up; our friend here got bit."

An audible moan of displeasure went up from the other hunters. For Hemingway, the hunt was 24/7, but the rest of the hunters had lives. They preferred to go on the hunt like any seasonal hunter would; after work, on weekends, and on vacations.

"Now, c'mon," said Milton. "That Shifter's just a level 2, barely aware of itself and what it can do. I already cut the arms and head off once."

"You had a level 2 decapitated, and you couldn't finish it?" snapped one of the hunters with a scar. "What the Hell's wrong with you guys?"

"It's my fault, Hugo," admitted Shelly. "Hem was trying to teach me."

"Yeah, don't pick on the intern," added Hem.

"My grandson's got a thing tonight; I can't go," said Wallace routinely.

"Yeah, the high school's doing a talent show," said another hunter. "My kid's in it too. Lots of folks are going."

"Well, what the Hell? This is a devil spawn we're talking about it!" insisted Hemingway. "You're just going to shirk your duty?!"

"Excuse me," said one particularly neatly dressed hunter with blond hair and a van dyke. "I believe it was **you** that broke all the rules, Hemingway."

"Oh, great," muttered Shelly.

"Who's that?" asked Lewis.

"Cousin Byron. He was Hem's intern a while back. He's not a fan," assured Shelly.

"We all have things to do, cuz," explained Byron. "All of Abe's Hat isn't at your beck and call every time you and Milton shake the bushes."

"C'mon, Byron," said Milton. "It's not like we called the thing out of the woods."

Hemingway looked away, appearing very guilty. Bryon crossed his arms in satisfaction. Milton turned towards Hemingway, looking betrayed.

"What did you do?"

"I, uh, **may** have tied a sprinkler to an R.C. car, filled it with human blood, and sent it in the woods to lure a devil out," admitted the hunter. "But it worked. **That's** the important thing."

"That's not the important thing at all! Jesus, Hem! Whose blood did you use?"

Hem cast a guilty toward one of the passed-out cousins in the corner of the lodge. The cousin snorted and let his hand fall toward the floor with a glass mug.

"Goddammit," muttered Milton.

"This is your mess; you clean it up," concluded Byron.

The other hunters, already fed up with Hem's antics over the years, agreed and left with Byron.

"We have a high school talent show to attend," added Byron smugly. "Happy hunting."

"C'mon, guys…" implored Milton, chasing after them. "Hem, you'd better start working on an apology barbecue!"

Hem made an annoyed grunt, then went behind the bar and poured himself an iced tea from the soda gun.

"Apology barbecue?" asked Lewis.

"Hem does a great brisket. Usually wins the lodge back when he cheeses them off," explained Shelly. "But we don't have 13 hours for you to slow roast meat!"

"Shelly," began Hem condescendingly, pouring iced teas for everyone. "You're standing in the presence of Abe Hat's number one devil hunter. The World's Greatest Hunter, in fact. I'm sure we can handle a level 2."

"Before it murders a bunch of people?"

"Define a bunch…."

20

"Hey, numbnuts," said Lewis, objecting. "All I wanted was directions to the gas station. I ain't goin' to prison cause **you're** an asshole."

"What do you expect me to do?"

"Go down into the sewer and kill it!" insisted Lewis.

Hem nearly did a spit take.

"That thing can shapeshift into an alligator or a crocodile or whatever else will eat you in a sewer. We can't follow it down there; that's suicide!"

"We're gonna have to use a book," said Shelly, moving toward the bookshelf.

"No-no-no! No books!" insisted Hem, rushing to the bookshelves and standing in front of it with his iced tea. "Do **not** open the books!"

"Why? Why is he afraid of books?" demanded Lewis.

"He doesn't like magic; it's not the actual books themselves."

"That's the dumbest thing I ever heard!" Lewis responded, reaching over the bar to add some bourbon to his iced tea. "You beat a demon---

"Devil."

"You beat a **devil** with a baseball bat; what's the big deal about using magic?"

"Wow, that was quick," said Hem to Shelly.

"I know. Lewis, you acclimate fast."

"Well, I just saw a demon---

"Devil."

"Whatever **head**, come to life!" said Lewis, backing away from one of the more ferocious-looking heads on the wall. "I have to assume that magic has some validity here! Now, which book do we need?"

"No, you don't understand," assured Hem. "There's always a **cost** to using magic. It's not like an instruction manual on your friggin' car!"

Lewis took a step toward the bookshelf, and Hem got in between.

"No. Do **not** open the books!"

"I'm lookin' at a book."

"No! We don't need them! What's my motto, Shelly?"

"Be prepared for any eventuality," she intoned, exasperated.

"Exactly, I've got six different backup plans at any one time. I've got more weapons hidden in my jacket than the cops got in four counties!"

"Oh, you're just the best, right?" said Lewis sarcastically. "That's why you let the thing get away?!"

Lewis tried to get past Hem to the bookshelves, and they struggled. It was one of those awkward fights where no one was particularly looking to hurt the other person. As the two wrestled, Shelly's phone rang, and she answered.

"Milton's got a solution," she announced. "Let's go."

"What solution?" asked Hem suspiciously.

"He's going to wake up Aunt Christie."

"Oh, no, he isn't!" insisted the hunter.

"Do you want to crack open a book or talk to your mother?"

"I think I'd rather just shoot myself," sighed Hem.

The devil head laughed through broken teeth. Hem threw his iced tea from across the room, and it smashed across the creature's face.

"Fine!" said the hunter.

Chapter 3

As the cousins left the lodge, something stirred in the sewers of Abe's Hat. The headless and armless demon floated in the dark muck, absorbing the filth. The dark vileness of the sewer's depths fed the creature's stumps until some tiny teeth grew. Some of the veins of the neck shot out, and the ends sprouted little maws; they grabbed a nearby rat and held it fast as the teeth drank the creature's blood hungrily. With each drop, its broken body repaired itself, growing a head that looked more and more like Lewis.

Even before the United States was a country, the Galloway Family Farm had been in the Galloway Family Farm. Generations of hunters had kept the place in pristine condition over the years, farming the land, raising chickens, and keeping the weeds at bay. But when it finally fell into Hemingway's hands, he was more hunter than farmer. While he put his most inventive and creative thoughts into the hunt, he'd always half-assed the farm stuff. Some of the other cousins had been on him to mow his front lawn, which was growing out of control. The only part that wasn't overgrown was the driveway and the short distance between that, the house, and the barn.

Hem's truck skidded to a halt outside the barn. He, Shelly, and Lewis jumped out.

"You guys sure you know what you're doin'?" asked Lewis. "Maybe we should call the cops or an exorcist."

"Oh, the Vatican **hates** us," said Shelly. "They've sent guys out here a bunch of times."

"Yeah," said Hem, annoyed at the thought. "It all ends the same way. A bunch of priests go screaming Italian into the woods and angry letters from the Pope about how we "staged" everything. No thanks."

"Is there anybody you haven't pissed off?" said Lewis, incredulous.

Hemingway thought a moment and then exhaled, "I'll have to get back to ya."

"Great! I get bit! I get shot! And the only guy that can help me lives with his mother!" lamented Lewis.

"Hey!" snapped Hemingway. "Technically, I don't **live** with my mother!"

"Well, I thought we were waking her up."

Hemingway handed Lewis a shovel.

"We are. Come around back."

The trio walked through the tall grass to the back of the farm. A few feet from the driveway, between the barn and the house, Milton was digging in the Galloway Family plot.

"Took you long enough," muttered Milton. "I don't know why you bother to cover her back up."

"Shut up! This isn't my idea! I thought you were going to talk to Byron!" Hemingway replied instantly.

"Byron has hated you ever since you embarrassed him at the carnival."

"It was part of a distraction; I was in the middle of a hunt!"

"And pantsing him in front of a crowd was part of that?!"

"Yes! The only one that didn't look at his dick was the devil spawn!"

"That's actually pretty clever," chuckled Lewis.

"See? He gets it."

"Can I ask a question, though? What are we doing here?" asked Lewis.

"Waking up, Aunt Christie. Didn't you tell him?" said Milton.

Milton's shovel hit something solid in the dirt. He and the others climbed out of the hole.

"Aunt Christie? Aunt Chris-teeeeee!" called Shelly.

"W-w-we're gonna talk to her spirit or s-something. R-r-right?" stammered Lewis, hoping it would be something less crazy than the hunting lodge.

"I only wish," said Hemingway annoyed. "Ma, get up; I need your help. C'mon ma. Ma? Maaaa!"

Suddenly, the lid of a coffin opened up under the dirt, and the dried corpse of a woman with stringy gray hair and a rotting nose rose up like in the silent movie with Nosferatu.

"Jesus Christ!" cried Lewis, horrified, dropping his shovel and stumbling back.

Aunt Christie opened her eyes and cackled. She was still wearing the rotting, black lace dress she loved to wear in life. On her feet were a distinctive pair of custom-made boots made from rattlesnake skin. The clasps had been silver, but someone had soldered bigger chunks of silver chains to them, then looped them around her ankles. These were anchored to what looked like a weighty block of cement.

"Hello, Hemmy! Oh, my little Hemmy, how I missed you," she said sweetly. "Come and give your mother a kiss."

Hemingway pointed at his mother and looked at Lewis.

"This is why you don't read the books," he explained.

"Oh, don't mind him," dismissed the old witch. "My Hemmy's an old stick in the mud. What's your name, cutie pie?"

"This is a friggin' amusement park ride," insisted Lewis, not quite accepting it. "You ain't real!"

"Oh, I'm real, baby," said Aunt Christie.

There was a brief flash, and Lewis found himself standing in the daylight talking to a very alive and sexy Aunt Christie. She had skin like alabaster and a black bra that highlighted the cleavage just above her Gypsy sundress. The locks of her raven hair danced about her shoulders as she leaned in to kiss Lewis.

But then there was another brief flash, and the old rotting crone was back. Lewis could see the maggots crawling in and out of her gums, and the foul stench of her rotting insides caused him to reel and wretch. Aunt Christie cackled, amused.

"Goddammit, ma!" snapped Hem, unable to take any more. "It's bad enough you won't die! You gotta embarrass me in front of my friends?! God! This is third grade all over again!"

"Aw, you never let me have any fun since I've been dead," said Aunt Christie slyly.

"Aunt Christie, our friend's here been bit. We need to locate the devil before it gets away," explained Milton.

Christie's eyes glowed bright green for a moment. She could see the devil's head almost entirely grown back and its stumpy arms regenerating in the sewer's muck.

"Yesssss," she hissed. "I see it. It's close. Gathering strength. In a short time, it will emerge, and it will hunger!"

Suddenly, the glow disappeared from her eyes.

"But what's in it for me?" she asked, mildly annoyed.

"What do you want?" asked Milton.

"Just take off these boots. Just for a few hours," she cooed innocently. "I promise I'll be a good girl."

"Not happening after last time," assured Milton.

"Oh, I thought you **liked** the boots, ma!" ranted Hemingway bitterly. "Maybe you should've spent that money on my 11th birthday like you promised! Maybe instead of banging that guy at the Renaissance Faire just to get silver clasps!"

"You exaggerate, Hemmy," she assured the group. "I paid for the clasps. The bootmaker was just hot."

"Yeah! And happy birthday to me, right?!"

"Jesus," muttered Lewis to Shelly. "If she wasn't already dead, I think your cousin would shoot her in the face."

"Hem isn't phased by much," Shelly muttered back. "But when it comes to his mother--- He just unravels."

"Just crawl back in the ground and rot already!" snapped Hem, pacing around like a cornered animal.

"If you want to save your friend, bring me my spellbook. I spent a lifetime accumulating my witchcraft. I should like to see it again," she requested.

Milton and Shelly stole a guilty glance toward Hemingway, who smiled. The hunter folded his arms in satisfaction, waiting for the other shoe to drop.

"Oh, shit," said Lewis, already anticipating the answer.

"Um, we can't. Hem burned it a week after you died," said Shelly sheepishly.

"WHAT?!"

The old witch grew in stature, her entire figure distorting into a monstrous visage. Her arms elongated, and her hands became bony claws.

"WHY?!" the old witch demanded.

"Because I told you I was gonna burn that thing after you died," laughed Hem. "I put in the fireplace and roasted some **God damned** s'mores!"

"Listen," said Lewis, trying to reason with the furious witch. "I'm not even with these guys. So if you could just do me a solid--- "

"You little **brat**! What is **wrong** with you?! I wish I had had a girl! A **girl** would've understood! A **girl** would've continued my legacy!" hissed the monstrous old crone. "Just like a man, you destroy everything you touch, Hem! Everything! That was my **life**! My **world**!"

"Yeah, well, you're **dead**! And in case you need reminding, maybe instead of reading spellbooks all day, you should've paid attention to your **kid** once in a while!" Hemingway ranted, still hurt. "Everyone in town's going to the high school talent show for their kid! *You never did that for me!"*

"Fine," said Aunt Christie, reverting back to normal size. "Sing for me then, Hemmy."

"What? Seriously?"

"If so important for you for me to see your act, then do it for me. Right here, right now, and I'll show you where the devil is," offered the witch.

"I don't know if I remember…" mumbled Hem, looking around and feeling cornered.

"That's a lie," assured Milton.

"Who side are you on, cuz?"

"Listen, man, I swear I won't laugh and won't judge," assured Lewis. "Just give the old broad what she wants."

Hemingway looked around, feeling a bit trapped by his own bravado. His mother sized him up. She knew he couldn't refuse her request. There was a lifetime of history between them, but whether this was going to be a good or bad moment was anyone's guess.

"Fine! You and Milton are my backup singers. Intern, start the truck, play disc 3, Track 1."

Shelly started up Hem's truck and drove it around to face the family plot. As Boston's *More Than a Feeling*, the lights backlit, her cousin played on the truck's stereo. Hemingway sang along with the lyrics, although he never even memorized all the words back in high school. He substituted several words he didn't understand with words he made up that sounded sorta similar, all while using the handle of his revolver as a microphone. Milton and Lewis sang back up, answering the chorus as Hem gyrated like the rockstar he used to imagine himself as a kid.

As the song faded, Hem dropped to his knees, a little spent but satisfied with his sing-along.

"Hmm," said Aunt Christie disdainfully. "Now you know why I didn't bother to go to your talent show."

Hem turned his gun around to blast his mother in the face, but Milton stopped him and pushed his hand down.

"Where's the devil, Aunt Christie?" demanded Milton.

The old witch's eyes glowed again, and the image of the devil lying in the muck appeared before them. The camera seemed to zoom out and back of the sewer to a street in Abe's Hat. Unfortunately, it was near mostly woods and a lone white mailbox.

"How the Hell are we supposed to find that? What's the address?" demanded Lewis.

Aunt Christie cackled uproariously. Hem broke free, but Milton had his revolver. The hunter picked up a shovel and smashed his dead mother in the face. He shoved her back towards the casket as she laughed with sinister glee.

"Get back in there! Get back!"

After a few hits and stomps, Hem had her back in her coffin. She continued to cackle the entire time.

"You'll never find it in time! You need magic! You're all going to die!" insisted the witch, holding her coffin lid open to taunt her son. "You should've learned, Hemingway. You should've listened to **your mother**!"

"Just stay dead, ma!" Hemingway insisted, slamming the lid. "Give me some peace of God damned mind!"

"Shelly, how many white mailboxes do you think there are in Abe's Hat?" asked Milton.

"Fifteen," she answered simply.

Milton looked impressed.

"Hem made me memorize stuff like that," she explained. "He said Batman knows Gotham, so I had to know Abe's Hat."

Milton turned toward Hem, who was frantically trying to rebury his mother.

"You made Shelly memorize the color of everyone's mailbox in town?"

"It came in useful, didn't it?"

"That's still a lot of mailboxes," said Milton. "How many of them are near a sewer like that?"

"I'm not sure," admitted Shelly. "Maybe four?"

"Jesus, can we talk about what just happened for a minute?!" demanded Lewis, overwhelmed by the events. "We just serenaded the Crypt Keeper's girlfriend!"

"Focus, Lewis, focus," insisted Milton. "Time's a bit of a factor here."

"Fine! I guess we each watch one mailbox," said Lewis.

"Lewis, no offense, but you cannot be by yourself," explained Milton. "All that devil has to do is kill you, and it will steal your whole identity."

"I can handle myself. Give me a gun," assured the gambler.

"You don't even know what to do!" snapped Hemingway, still burying.

"You can't shoot a devil with regular bullets; it just annoys them. You gotta use silver-tipped bullets and weapons," explained Shelly. "Then, once you've got it incapacitated, you gotta cut out its heart."

"What?! You guys didn't tell me that! What the Hell does that look like?"

"About what you'd expect. Lots of screaming and a fountain of black blood," said Milton, remembering. "The screaming's bad. I took to wearing earplugs."

28

"Now, I **really** want a gun."

Hemingway staggered back to the group, a little out of breath. He threw aside his shovel and pulled out a road map.

"Let's do this smart," announced Hem. "Where are the mailboxes?"

Shelly took out a pen and marked them on a map. Two of them were about a block apart.

"Oh, this'll be easy," concluded Hem. "These two are pretty close; I'll take them. Milton, you take the one at the edge of the woods; Shelly and Lewis watch the last one."

"How are you going to watch two sewer drains at the same time?" asked Milton.

"I'll just turn my head back and forth? Duh!"

"Cuz, that thing is fast. It's going to be a level 3 by the time it crawls out of there," said Shelly, worried for him.

"Look, we'll all get on the cellphones; first one to spot anything calls the others," explained Hem.

"I don't like this plan," said Milton. "Just go apologize to Byron."

"There's no time, now. The sun goes down in twenty minutes," insisted the hunter. "Look, we can do this. Everyone use a deer stand and stay frosty."

Back at the high school, one of the cousin's kids was dancing to a Katy Perry song with three classmates as backup. Somewhere in the audience, Byron was sitting next to Wallace and glanced at his smartphone.

"Still no apology?" asked Wallace.

"From Hemingway? Not a chance," said Byron knowingly. "I'd rather have the brisket anyway."

Chapter 4

At the mailboxes, Milton was hiding in a deer stand, swords ready. Hemingway decided he needed to be closer to the ground. He stood with his back against a tree, gun in each hand, checking both ways. Finally, in another tree, Shelly and Lewis watched a lone sewer grate together from another deer stand. Lewis's phone buzzed. It was Pete. He immediately sent it to voice mail.

"So what do you do outside of this?" asked Lewis. "I know you ain't a professional crossbow shooter."

"Oh, ha-ha. Now you sound like one of my cousins. I run a custom tire and rim shop, but I also draw comics."

"No, shit? So you're an artist?"

"Not really, just for fun. And you're a professional card shark?"

"Poker player, yeah. I win tournaments and prizes and junk."

"Really? Like the World Series of Poker?"

"Oh, well, ya know--- Something like that," said Lewis, scrambling to change the subject. "But how'd you get caught up in all this demon---"

"Devil," corrected Shelly.

"Get caught up in this devil stuff?"

"It's kind of a family thing," said Shelly, shrugging. "My cousins were always talking about it. Going on hunting trips."

"You make it sound like nothing! This is some crazy shit you guys do in the woods! I don't know if I could do it."

"I grew up with it, so I guess it's no big deal to me."

"Well, I appreciate what you and your cousins are doing. Seriously, you're lucky to have that kind of family. I'd like to thank you. You know, over drinks and dinner," said Lewis smoothly.

Shelly laughed despite herself.

"Uh, huh. Can I bring Hem?"

"Absolutely not!"

The couple laughed. It had been a while since Shelly had dated anyone. Hemingway's training regime had tied up her nights and weekends for months. The only other guy she had been interested in at that time was a New Jersey State Trooper the cousins had saved from a Level 5 Soul Reaper, but after the officer pissed his pants in the middle of the fight, she had changed her mind.

"It's kinda weird that he's your cousin," said Lewis. "Seems more like he'd be your uncle."

"When I was a kid, I called him Uncle Hem," she admitted. "God, I think that was like 15 years ago."

"What was?" asked Lewis.

Lewis had read somewhere that making physical contact with a woman during a conversation was essential to let you know you were interested. Unfortunately, this sent him another vision when he put his hand on her thigh.

Shelly, 10 years old and fresh from the bus out of Abe's Hat Elementary, was walking home with her Billy & Mandy backpack. As she walked down the dirt path towards her house in the Pines, she heard something scuttling in the brushes. Worried, she increased speed. After a few steps, whatever was stalking her started breathing heavy and growling. Shelly broke out into a run, and then suddenly, a creature jumped in front of her.

Half-wolf, part-horse with red skin and horns, it opened its maw of fangs and growled at the little girl. Shelly just stood there, unsure of what to do. Before the creature could bite her, a bear trap projectile came sailing out of the woods and struck the beast in the mouth. The trap had snapped shut before hitting the fiend, and it reeled in pain. Hemingway, in his prime, stepped out of the woods with a young Byron trailing after him.

"Dammit, that didn't work!" complained the hunter. "Grab the kid!"

The devil, a level 7 Flesh Render, shook off the hit and returned to attacking Shelly. Hemingway smacked the fiend in the side of its head with a heavily dented metal softball bat, and Byron pulled Shelly away from the creature. The devil roared in pain and annoyance. Before it could recover, Hemingway shot it in the face. It collapsed on the ground, moaning in pain.

"Hey, you're Shelly?" guessed Hemingway. "Carrie's kid, right?"

"Should she really be seeing this?" suggested Byron, wanting to protect Shelly from the gruesome spectacle.

"Dude! Look at her! She's not even phased! You're a brave little girl, Shel," said the hunter, impressed.

Hemingway pushed a knife into the Flesh Render's shoulder and pinned it against a tree. It moaned pitifully, and when it tried to reach up to claw at Hemingway, he fired his revolver blowing off its other arm. It exploded, sending black blood and viscera everywhere. Some of it got splashed across Shelly's face, but she didn't seem bothered by it.

"Jesus, Hem!" objected Byron.

"Look at her!" said Hem. "Nerves of God damned steel! That's Galloway blood, Byron! That's a Galloway!"

Shelly touched the black blood with her hand and looked at it curiously. She wasn't actually that brave; the entire event had mildly traumatized her. Fortunately, her folks could afford a shrink.

"When you're old enough, Shelly," said Hemingway. "You come to find me. I'll teach you to hunt. You're definitely on my list of potential interns."

"Thanks, Uncle Hem."

"You can definitely learn something from this one, Byron."

"Seriously?" said Byron, feeling wholly disrespected. "She's like **ten**."

"That's your problem, Byron," insisted the hunter as he continued to cut into the moaning devil as black blood spurted everywhere. "You don't open your **mind** to things."

"Lewis? You okay? You drifted away for a minute," said Shelly.

"Yeah-yeah, fine," said Lewis, now back in the present. "You ever get, like, **dreams** when you're wide awake?"

"Like daydreams?" asked Shelly, not really understanding.

"Yeah," said Lewis. "Only you're in them, and they're about stuff that actually happened."

"Like a flashback in your own life, sure," agreed Shelly.

"What about…other people's lives?" asked Lewis carefully. "You ever get like a **vision**. Something that happened, but you weren't there for, but you totally know that's what happened."

"So you're saying you're psychic?"

"No!" dismissed Lewis. "That's stuff is--- It's ridiculous. I don't believe in any of that stuff. No, you totally misunderstand."

"What do you believe in?"

"You know, after the last 12 hours or so," Lewis admitted. "I don't know. But you seem like a decent person. I mean, you **shot** me…."

"I am still so sorry about that, by the way."

"But you bandaged me up and helped me," said Lewis. "So we're good, but you could still have dinner with me. Ya know, to reward me for being a sport."

"I'm thinking about it," blushed Shelly. "Let's just make sure you're safe first, okay? I don't want one of my cousins shooting off your pinky finger in the middle of dinner just to be sure you're human."

Lewis laughed.

"Because they will not let us back in that restaurant again," said Shelly, finishing the story.

When Lewis realized Shelly wasn't joking, his expression morphed from joking to concerned.

Chapter 5

Back at the first mailbox, Milton watched while pulling out his cellphone. He called Hem. Hemingway had already strapped his smartphone to his jacket. He tapped the button, putting it on speaker as he looked left and right every few seconds.

"How's it going, cuz?"

"Well, my neck's getting a little sore, but otherwise fine," assured Hemingway. "I'm gonna finish off this Level 3 shit stain."

"Don't be a hero. We already screwed this up once. I worry about you."

"Me? I worry about you. Dating Joyce? Weren't you already seeing that chick from the toll booth?"

"Ah, that wasn't going anywhere," assured Milton.

"Really? Seems like always having plenty of change would be a plus," joked Hem. "Or were you just sick of banging her that fast?"

"Cuz, it's not like that."

"Yeah, right. You're lucky the GPS on your phone doesn't have a blacklight mode. Your DNA is probably on half the county!"

"That's a bit of an exaggeration!" laughed Milton.

Hem, who was laughing at his own joke, hesitated a bit on the neck turning. Remembering, he turned suddenly and was looking into the eyes of Lewis.

"Oh shit!"

Hem's phone cut out, and Milton immediately went running, calling Shelly as he did. At the same time, the fake Lewis had slapped Hemingway hard enough to throw him out of the woods and onto the road. The impact caused the hunter to drop his guns. He instantly regretted not adding more padding in his jacket. It was full of the various weapons and gadgets he had squirreled away for devil hunting.

"Ow," moaned Hemingway. "Really should've tucked and rolled on that one."

The Devil Lewis stomped over to Hemingway, walking right past his revolver. The creature was still relishing an opportunity to tear apart a live human for its amusement. It picked up Hemingway by the scruff of his jacket.

"You shot me!" it growled.

"Then you're not gonna like this."

Hemingway sprayed the devil in the face with a mister bottle of holy water. It was like acid on the creature's face. It threw the hunter aside, but he remembered to tuck and roll this time. The devil spawn howled in pain.

"Ow. The tuck and roll didn't help," moaned Hemingway on the asphalt.

Down the street, Milton was running in their direction, swords drawn. Shelly and Lewis were running from the other direction.

"Hem!" called Milton.

"We're coming, cuz!" shouted Shelly, firing off a crossbow bolt.

The bolt completely missed the creature, bounced on the road, and knocked away one of Hemingway's guns as he reached for it.

"Dammit, Shelly!"

"Sorry!"

The devil turned toward Lewis and smiled.

"Lewis! Stay back!" shouted Milton.

The hellspawn started to take a few steps toward Lewis, but Hemingway got to his feet and jumped on its back. He locked his hands together so the monster couldn't throw him off immediately.

"Daniel-san! Sweep the legs!" shouted Hem as Milton reached them.

Milton slid feet first on his ass, avoiding a wild swing from the devil, and cut it off at the knees. It howled in pain and fell over. Unfortunately, it started rolling back toward the storm drain. Hemingway stopped himself, but the creature rolled into the dark storm drain.

"Oh, great!" snapped the hunter. "How badly you gonna keep screwing this up, guys? I mean, could this be any--- "

At that moment, the creature reached out of the drain, grabbed Hemingway by the feet, and pulled him into the drain before the cousins could react. He scrambled for his gun or a handhold but slid into the drain.

"Shelly-don't-follow-me-down-here!" he managed to shout on the way down.

Milton got up and threw his jacket off, preparing to follow him down.

"Milton, no!"

"Just stay up here, Shelly. Watch Lewis."

"But he said it was suicide to go down there!" added Lewis.

"Hem says a lot of things. Shelly, tell Lewis the codeword," added Milton before sliding into the darkness after his cousin.

"Codeword?"

"A lot of the devils are shifters, so you have to have a codeword in case one of us gets replaced," explained Shelly, getting out her smartphone and starting the app. "We all have the app that generates the word. It's apparently rotten banana."

"Okay, rotten banana," repeated Lewis.

"Oh, crap! There's an update. Shit, now it's pink parasol."

"Well, we'll just say both."

"You can't just **say** the codeword; that's a dead giveaway. You have to use them organically in a sentence, so the devil doesn't realize you're testing it."

"How the Hell am I supposed to make a sentence like that?!"

"I don't know!"

"Look, Shel', your cousins are cool and all, but I think they're over their heads here. We gotta take matters into our own hands," said Lewis.

Lewis started walking. Shelly chased after him.

"No-no-no! I have to watch you!"

"Then c'mon!"

Back in the sewer, Hemingway had lost the devil in the darkness. He opened up a pocket in his jacket, Velcro-ed a small flashlight to his hat, and pulled out a Glock he had taped up in a plastic bag for this very occasion. Hemming way walked along the ledge of the sewer, kicking the rats away as he did so.

"Cuz?"

He found Milton as he rounded a corner. He had hurt himself jumping down into the storm drain, or so Hem thought.

"Milton, I told you not to come down here."

"I think I broke my ankle; help me up."

"Yeah, your bones are about as strong as a rotten banana," said Hem.

"What's that supposed to mean?"

"Ah, ha! You're the devil spawn! You got the word wrong!"

"There was an update, you dumbass! Check your phone."

Hem pulled out his phone to check for the update, but that brief distraction gave the fiend just enough time to jump on Hemingway. He fell back and dropped his gun into the inky back muck of the sewer. The creature bit down on his forearm as Hem moved to block the bite, and there was a loud clank. The creature howled.

"Ow! My fucking teeth!" it growled.

"Silver armbands, shit stain!" said Hemingway rolling up his sleeve.

The creature turned around, pushed Hemingway down, and ripped open one of his pant legs. He didn't have any protection there. The creature moved to bite him. Fortunately, Hemingway's backup was his Taxi Driver-esque sleeve gun. The Dillinger slid out into his hand, and Hem blasted the devil in the face. The creature reeled and fell backward into the darkness. The bullet struck a metal ladder some distance away, causing a spark; the spark ignited the methane, and a wall of flame shot back down the sewer at Hem.

"Oh, shit."

Hemingway dove into the muck just as a wave of heat zoomed over him. Unfortunately, it was right near a nexus of pipes, and he found himself getting sucked down into the water through another pipe and floating along toward the grate to outside.

"Okay," said Hemingway. "Prepared for any eventuality."

Hemingway had a small blowtorch in a plastic bag, which he immediately pulled out and ignited. He figured he could cut open a big enough hole in the grate and follow the water out. When his feet hit it, the entire rusty grate came off the sides of the pipe, and Hem

36

immediately tumbled into a nearby drainage lake. Soaking wet, he crawled out of the lake and threw the blow torch aside.

"I am spending a shit ton of money at the hardware store for **nothing**!"

Back in the sewer, Milton had chased the devil down the wrong passage. When Hem's gun went off, he backed into a depression in the side of the sewer, which was convenient for when the ignited methane zoomed past his feet. The edges of his pant legs ignited, but with a sword in each hand, he was forced to put them back into the scabbards on his back. He beat out the flames with his hands while watching for the inevitable ambush. Hem, soaking wet, came around the corner impatient.

"What the Hell, Milton? You just gonna stand there beating your pants all night?"

"What happened to you?"

"I fell down some pipes," dismissed the hunter. "It's like Mario World down here. Gimme a sword."

"Why don't you use your pink parasol to fight the devil?"

"Pink parasol? What the Hell are you talking about? We're gonna get eaten down here!"

"Dammit, Hem! I told you there was an update on the app," said Milton tossing him a sword.

The second the sword hit the air, Milton saw Hem's expression change. He knew he had made a mistake. The devil had managed a tiny bite on Hem's leg; the hunter was now only just discovering. Fortunately for Milton, his recent parkour classes and his many years of ballet as a kid made him quick and flexible enough to dodge a sword. Milton flipped backward, rolled into the sewer water, and then came up in a different spot as the fake Hem swung into the muck. Milton brought the sword down on the devil's wrist, severing the hand that held the sword. It squealed like an animal and fled into the darkness.

"Hem!" called Milton. "Cuz?!"

Lewis had insisted on heading back to the hunting lodge, and Shelly reluctantly drove him there. She thought he would plead his case to the rest of the cousins, but he marched right up to Lee.

"Lee, you gotta let us in the back," insisted Lewis. "It's an emergency."

"I haven't done the test," said Lee. "I'm not doing that."

"Shelly, get me back there?"

"No," insisted Lee. "You don't have Hem to bully me, and he's not a cousin, so he don't get in."

"How do you **know** I'm not a cousin? I lived in South Philly all my life, and that's right across the river. I could be a relative."

"At least look up his name," asked Shelly. "What's your last name, Lewis?"

"Cognata."

Lee pulled out thick, leather-bound books with the lineage of the Galloway family and the extended family.

"Why didn't you do that last time?!" said Lewis.

"DNA is actually faster. This book goes back over 250 years," explained Lee. "There is an extension of the Cognata Family. Was your grandmother's name Florence?"

"I had a great aunt by that name. Good enough?"

"It's a start...."

"Look, Hem and Milton went into the sewer to get the devil spawn. The whole hunt has gone to Hell. Let us go talk to some cousins in the back. Please, cuz," pleaded Shelly. "You know Hem doesn't mean half the stuff he says."

Lee sighed, resigned.

"Can we see last year's hunting trophies, please?" asked Shelly.

Lee opened the secret passage, and the couple ducked behind the fireplace. The back was empty. Lewis marched right up to the first bookcase, looking for a way to open it.

"What the Hell are you doing?!" demanded Shelly, realizing he was going for a book.

"I'm getting a book. One's got a spell or something, right?" said Lewis. "How do you open this?"

"Not that case!"

Inside the case, one of the books suddenly started to flutter around when Lewis touched the glass. One splayed itself on the inside of the glass, exposing its demonic mouth with equally demonic teeth. Startled, Lewis reeled back and stumbled against a table, knocking over an empty mug as he did so.

"Christ Almighty! What the Hell is that?!"

"Yeah, those books come to life, or they're devils. No one's really sure. The glass for that case was made with silver, so they can't get out," explained Shelly casually. "You don't want those books. In fact, this whole thing is a bad idea. We can't even touch them without Cousin Eliot's permission."

"Who's Eliot?"

Eliot, the same cousin that Hemingway had siphoned blood out of earlier, walked out of the shadows of the Lodge from the restroom. He was an older cousin, maybe 60-something, but Eliot was a hardy 60-something with a close-cropped gray afro and glasses. He had a jacket on from the Poolside Resort Casino in Atlantic City.

"Shelly, who's this man touching my bookcases?" demanded Eliot.

"Eliot, this is Lewis. He was here earlier when you were passed out."

"Look, your cousins are in the sewer. They could already be dead. We gotta try and help 'em!" insisted Lewis. "Don't give it to me; give it to Shelly."

"Me? I can't look at a book. I swore to Hem I wouldn't," said Shelly. "And he wasn't kidding when he said there's a price."

"Anything's better than going to prison; I'll do it. I'll be fine," insisted Lewis. "Now, which book?"

Shelly sighed, resigned.

"You don't even know what you're doing," said Eliot. "You think the devils are bad? I've seen some of these books twist a hunter's brain inside out. We got more than one cousin in Ancora."

"The nuthouse?" asked Lewis, a little worried. "No offense, old-timer, but this family could have its own wing."

"If a book don't kill you, using one too much could make you wish it did," warned Eliot. "Hemingway's mother--- "

"Yeah, we met. I'm not a fan," said Lewis impatiently.

"Well, I ain't a fan of being called old," assured Eliot.

"I see by your jacket you're a gambling man. What say you play me a hand of Texas Hold 'em? I beat you; you let me have a book to help the boys," offered Lewis. "I mean unless you're too old to play."

"I'm not even that old--- What is with you?" demanded Eliot. "And I've been gambling since before I went to 'Nam. What do I get if I win?"

"How about a grand?" offered Lewis, pulling out one of the stacks of money Pete had given him for the tournament. "Seems fair for a book."

"This doesn't seem right," said Shelly, uncomfortable. "Eliot's always had a problem with…control."

"Pff! Fine with me. It's his funeral," said the defensive Eliot sitting down and tossing a deck of cards on the table.

Lewis shuffled them, letting the cards dance a bit over his fingers. Pulling something over casino players and in some of the backroom games he played--- That was almost impossible. But in this room, all he had to decide was how badly he wanted to beat Eliot. After a quick deal, it was all over. Lewis's eights and fours beat out Eliot's pair of kings.

"Move three shelves over. Any one of those might be helpful," he revealed. "Don't tell Hem I let you."

Lewis counted three books shelves over and found one that clearly had two doors and a latch. He chose a book that looked like it was bound with bark and deerskin.

"This isn't written on human flesh or nothin', right?" asked Lewis, picking up the book.

"Well, not **that** one," said Shelly. "But it's old. Real old. The Indians called it the Walam Olum."

"What's that mean? Spellbook?"

"No one knows. I don't think that's going to help much since it was written over 12,000 years ago in a language no one speaks anymore, by a culture that didn't have written language," explained Eliot. "Now, if you'll excuse me."

"Aren't you gonna help us?" asked Lewis.

"Uh-huh," said Eliot as he exited. "I'm going to find my cousins or what's left of 'em if the devil got 'em."

Lewis flipped through the rough pages. There were symbols he didn't understand, but at the edge of his hearing, he could hear whispers.

"Do you hear that?" asked Lewis.

"Hear what?" said Shelly. "Wait. What do you hear?"

"Whispers. They're trying to tell me something. Tell me how to get the devil," Lewis said to the whispers.

"Lewis, please, just put it back," begged Shelly.

"Relax, I'm fine."

"Lewis, you're **not** fine."

"Why?"

Shelly turned on her smartphone, turned the camera around so it was taking pictures of the user, and then showed the screen to Lewis. His eyes were glowing bright green.

"W-w-w-well I don't feel weird or anything. Should I be worried?" said Lewis, extremely worried. "Cause I'm not scared if this is the sort of thing that normally happens. Is it?"

Shelly was being a bit wishy-washy and knew she shouldn't. She knew she should've slapped the book out of Lewis's hands when he picked it up. But she kinda liked Lewis and was worried it would put the kibosh on their "vibe." But now, Lewis's skull was lit up like a Christmas tree.

Just as she was about to tell him to put the book back, Lewis started speaking in a strange ancient tongue. In a deepened voice, Lewis began to chant as if possessed by some ancient shaman spirit. Shelly knew using the was dangerous, and if her cousin found out about it, Shelly would be in big, big trouble.

However, she had never been so turned on in her life.

Lewis staggered and, in trying to regain his balance, placed his hand on one of the mounted demonic heads. The plaque read "Milton Galloway" and had a date from the '90s. When Lewis's hand touched the head, it began to moan in pain. There was a flash from Lewis' hand, and the devil head began to scream. It collapsed in on itself, making bone-crunching noises as it did. When Lewis lifted his hand up, he was clutching a demonic-looking dagger. His eyes stopped glowing.

"Holy shit! I think you were right, Shelly! I shouldn't'veshouldn't've messed with--- "

Unfortunately, Shelly wasn't paying attention. She leaped onto Lewis and started kissing him hard.

Back in the sewer, Hemingway had found one of his revolvers and went back down. He rounded a corner and was suddenly in a stand-off with Milton.

"Milton," he greeted cautiously.

"Cuz," said Milton, just as cautious.

"You know, I hope you didn't get sick on that banana bread; I used **rotten bananas**," said the hunter deliberately.

"That's how you use a code word? You're supposed to be subtle, and you didn't update your app again," insisted Milton.

"Dammit, another update?"

"Yeah."

"Well, let's just do this the easy way. Cut me," insisted Hem.

Milton slashed Hemingway across the palm. He held up his bloody hand for confirmation.

"Okay, see?" said Hem.

Hem cocked the hammer back on his revolver.

"Now, you--- "

"Wait-wait-wait! What the Hell are you doing?"

"I was going to shoot you."

"You could kill me, you idiot!"

"No!" assured Hemingway. "I'll just graze you."

"You don't have that kind of accuracy! No one does!" pointed out Milton. "And didn't you ignite the gas down here last time?"

"That's true. Fine. Gimme a sword."

"I can't. It's the only other weapon I have down here now. Give me the gun."

"There is no way I'm giving you the gun! You could be the devil!"

"If I was the devil, I would've cut your hand off when you put it up for me to cut!"

Hem thought about that for a moment. That was a valid point.

"Still, though. Even with one hand, I got the gun. That's a clear tactical advantage," noted Hemingway. "Besides, Cousin Mel killed that Level 9 Eye-eater after it bit off his hand, and they just sewed it back on."

"Mel was in the hospital for six months! He's still going to rehab!" insisted Milton. "He told me he can't feel two fingers. I think you just want to shoot me."

"Well, not to **hurt** you. Just to make a point," admitted Hemingway.

"What kind of point is that?!"

"That you are a bit sword-obsessed. There. I said it."

"Don't start."

"It's true, Mil. You're a police officer, for God's sake. You should hunt with a gun!"

"Swords are quiet."

"Guns are quiet until you blow somebody's head off," assured Hem. "Makes no sense. If you hunted with a gun, you'd be a better hunter and probably a better cop."

"You got too many opinions! Ya know that, Hem?" said Milton, finally sick of his nonsense. "Just because you're good at hunting devils doesn't mean you know everything!"

"Well, excuse me for being a little older and wiser! Maybe if you weren't banging every available chick in a 50-mile radius, you would've learned something more than the best stores to buy condoms!"

"Oh! I should be like you? Spending my weekends at Happy Hand Massage?!"

"Maybe a happy ending would clear your head before you jumped into another doomed relationship!"

"At least I'm capable of a relationship!"

Hem and Milton had been inching closer and closer with each exchange. Milton was about an arm's length away, while Hemingway whipped out a water pistol and sprayed Milton in the mouth while he said "relationship." It made it come out like "relation shit." Milton gagged a little, and it had hit the back of his throat.

"What the Hell was that?" he demanded.

"It's another devil test I devised, so I can't tell you, but we'll know in a sec."

Milton vomited into the sewer.

"Oh, my God," he said after retching. "Was that--- Ipecac?!"

"Yeah, sorry. Devil's don't react to it; I figured it would be a good test."

"Why didn't you just spray me with the holy water?!"

"You gotta keep your quarry on their toes, Mil. We gotta mix it up."

Milton vomited again, this time all over his shoes.

"Ooo, sorry," apologized Hemingway. "But at least we can get out of the sewer now."

"Hem," said Milton trying not to dry heave. "The devil bit you. It can look like you, and it's not **here**."

"Shit! Shelly," said Hem, suddenly remembering.

Chapter 6

Back at the Lodge, Shelly's phone was buzzing in a pile of clothes. She and Lewis had had a brief but intense sexual encounter behind the bar. Lewis stood up, out of breath, and poured some shots.

"Damn, baby. That was hot," said Lewis, handing Shelly a shot glass and clinking. "Did I cast some kind of sex spell on you or what?"

"I don't think so," said Shelly. "At least, I hope not."

"Well, what am I supposed to do with this?" he asked, placing the evil-looking dagger on the bar.

The dagger was pure black with no sheen to it at all. It was only about half an inch thick and six inches long but felt almost as heavy as a sword. It had weird tiny protrusions sticking out of the ends of the handle and the blade. So flat, it seemed virtually two-dimensional. With all the small protrusions, the blade looked like a profile of the mounted devil head screaming.

"We should probably tell the boys," admitted Shelly. "Hem's going to be so pissed."

"Then screw it. I said I wanted to get the devil; this knife will let me do that, right? I could find it, stab, and boom! No more devil!"

"But it's not silver," said Shelly, thinking it through. "But it is magic, I guess?"

"It's made out of another devil. They can't be immune to that!" assured Lewis. "It would be like me being immune to punching myself."

"That's not an accurate analogy."

"Whatever," said Lewis, dismissing it and getting dressed. "We go back, save your cousins, kill this thing, and hit the tables at Caesar's. Bada boom, bada bing."

At an intersection in Abe's Hat, Eliot drove his El Camino toward the reservoir where he'd hope to find the two cousins and not their two corpses. Hemingway stepped out of the trees near a stop sign.

44

"You'd better get over to the Lodge, Hem. Shelly's flipping through books with that guy that got bit," said Eliot.

Hemingway continued to stare at him.

"Shit," muttered Eliot, realizing it wasn't him.

Eliot jammed the accelerator and turned toward the creature, but it jumped onto the hood. It smashed a bloody stump through the windshield. Eliot backed away as much as his car seat would let him while trying to reach his shotgun in the back seat. The creature's veins began to slowly stretch out. The tiny mouths full of demonic teeth at the end of the severed black veins hungered for his blood. With his right hand, Eliot flipped up the armrest, exposing a custom switch, and flipped it. The hood, which was springloaded to open away from the windshield, flung the surprised devil into the woods. It sailed into the trees, smacked against a trunk, and scurried into the darkness. Eliot got his shotgun and stepped out of the El Camino just as the real Hemingway and Milton came running up.

"Was that it?" asked Milton.

"Wait a minute," Hem said cautiously.

"Pink parasol," Eliot immediately said.

"That wasn't even a sentence," Hem muttered. "But that was it?"

"Yeah," said Eliot, disgusted that he hadn't been quick enough to shoot it.

"Holy shit! The hood worked!" said Hemingway proudly. "I told you that was a good install! Shelly did a good job!"

"Except that now I have to replace my hood and my windshield, Hem," reminded Eliot. "That's like $500!"

"Well, at least you don't have to replace your **face**, El! Thanks to **my** intern!" snapped Hem. "You can't argue with a good install!"

"If I wasn't a quart low of blood, I might've gotten to my shotgun in time, you turd!"

"Don't call me a turd, Eliot!" snapped Hem.

"Cousins, c'mon," reminded Milton. "We're all on the same side. We gotta keep this devil from escaping town!"

"I'll get Shelly to reinstall your stupid hood," said Hem reluctantly. "Sorry, Uncle El."

Technically, Hemingway was Eliot's second cousin, but when he was a kid, he had called him uncle. He called him that now to show that he meant no disrespect.

"Can you please drive over to the high school? The talent show should be just about done. Maybe convince some of the cousins to help?" asked Hemingway. "Not that we couldn't use you on the hunt, but--- "

"Yeah, all right," said Eliot. "Sorry I called you a turd."

"You're all right, El," smiled Hem, giving him a hug.

"Oh and, uh, Shelly and that fella that got bit are back at the Lodge flipping through some of the books," added Eliot, realizing he hadn't told the real Hem.

Hem quickly transitioned from manly hug to interrogating a suspect. He grabbed Eliot by the lapels and pushed him against the truck.

"Have you lost your God damned mind?! Shelly's not to read those books! You're supposed to be the librarian, Eliot!" insisted Hem.

"Well, I don't like to censor people. Seems very anti-librarian," Eliot replied, a little torn. "He beat me in a hand of Texas Hold 'em."

"You bet access to the books?" asked Milton. "You got a problem, cuz."

Milton pulled Hemingway away from Eliot.

"What's going to convince you the books are dangerous, Eliot?! You want to stop by the farm so that my undead mother can take a bite out of your brain?!"

Eliot paused and then said something he instantly regretted.

"Your mother was always nice to me."

Hemingway lurched toward Eliot, grabbing him by the throat.

"I meant that she was polite! That's all!"

"Let him go, Hem!" insisted Milton.

Milton dragged Hemingway off toward the Lodge.

"Get to the high school and bring everyone you can back to the Lodge. Make sure you remind them Hemingway and Lewis are bit," instructed Milton.

"And don't stop to buy rub-offs," added Hemingway.

"I do **not** have a gambling problem!" insisted Eliot.

Eliot found a beer on the floor of his truck and popped the top.

"God damn lecture every time," muttered Eliot before taking a sip.

By the time Hemingway and Milton reached the outskirts of the Lodge, they spotted Lewis and Shelly driving away. Hemingway was a little winded from running the six blocks.

"Shit, where are they going?" he panted.

"Back to save us. Where do you think?" answered Milton, pulling out his phone.

Hemingway aimed his revolver at a tree, but the shot was a dud.

"Dammit, I'm waterlogged!"

"Yeah, my phone's dead. Do we wait for the Lodge or go after them?"

Still breathless, Hemingway shrugged and started heading back to the sewer grate. Milton followed. The other cousins would just have to find them.

In the truck, Shelly sped back toward the white mailboxes and sewer grates. Lewis spotted a bloody Hemingway, dragging himself along the sandy floor of the Pine Barrens.

"Jesus Christ, is that him?"

Shelly stopped the truck.

"Not sure. Approach with extreme caution," she warned.

Lewis stepped out with the dagger in hand. Shelly wound the crossbow, loaded a bolt, and aimed at the bloody hunter.

"Hem, don't be mad, but Lewis borrowed one of the books," she taunted.

"Rot…ten…bananas," Hemingway managed to say with a mouthful of blood.

"Oh, God. That's the password!" said Shelly, lowering her crossbow. "Hem, is that you? What happened?"

"Wait a minute, Shel," warned Lewis, still suspicious.

But before Lewis could stop her, Shelly had moved forward to help the fake Hemingway. The creature pointed its bloody stump toward Shelly, shooting the little veins with tiny mouths in her direction. They latched onto her face and immediately began drinking her blood. In a panic, Shelly screamed and dropped the crossbow.

"Shelly!" shouted Lewis, charging forward with the dagger.

About two blocks away, Hemingway and Milton heard the scream. Milton increased his pace, and Hemingway was too out of shape to keep up.

Fortunately for Shelly, Lewis had always been a scrapper. Using the dagger, he sliced the veins, severing the connection between the devil and Shelly. Then he grabbed the fake Hemingway, whose face was already becoming distorted and more devil-like, and stabbed it in the chest. It struggled impotently for a few moments, then collapsed.

Furious at the thing that had bit Shelly, Lewis cut open the chest and prepared to cut out the creature's heart. But as soon as he cut into the beast's heart, the dagger seemed to absorb the heart and black blood. The fiend, who had returned to its natural devil-like state, quickly expired.

A bright orange, red and black portal spontaneously opened near the devil's corpse. It was spinning in a spiral pattern drawing the air and anything light enough towards its center. Leaves and twigs were caught up in its winds but burst into flame the instant they touched it. The wind in the portal to Hell was loud, like a dying, rickety airplane engine combined with an angry cat.

"Lewis! Hang on!" screamed Shelly, grabbing his hand.

Shelly had already stuck her other arm under a nearby tree root. Lewis watched as the creature's body as it was slowly pulled into the portal.

"Oh, wait. Trophy!" Lewis shouted over the wind.

Lewis cut off the head of the devil with the dagger in one swift move but, in the process, lost his grip. The dagger was pulled by the wind towards the portal, but the gambler managed to hold onto the devil's head. The portal sucked in the headless corpse of the devil and abruptly disappeared. The dagger landed somewhere in the darkness of the woods.

"Oh, my God, I can't believe that worked," said Shelly.

One of the creature's veiny appendages still dangled off Shelly's chin. Lewis gently pulled it off and looked into her eyes.

"I'm glad you're okay. Be a shame to ruin that pretty face of yours," said Lewis smoothly.

Shelly blushed and bit her bottom lip. She was about to kiss him when Milton suddenly arrived on the scene, trailed by Hemingway.

48

"Interrupting something?" Milton said suspiciously.

"Lewis killed it!" Shelly said excitedly, getting on her feet.

"What? No way," smiled Milton, relieved.

"Wait a minute!" said Hemingway, now almost wheezing. "That's about as believable as…(wheeze!)…a pink parasol."

Lewis held up the devil's head by one of its horns.

"This is a stupid app," Hem suddenly insisted. "We should just go back to a clipboard in the Lodge."

"I am really impressed, Lewis," Milton gushed. "Some of the cousins still haven't made a first kill."

"I'm going to get one," assured Shelly. "I get an assist."

"An assist is excellent for an intern," added Hem, finally catching his breath. "Wait a minute. Where's the book? Did you open a book?!"

"Yeah, I couldn't read it, though," assured Lewis, handing it back. "I mean, how could I, right?"

Hemingway snatched the old tome out of Lewis's hands, eyeing him warily.

"Did you look at this?" he demanded from Shelly.

"No, but--- "

"She said she promised you that she wouldn't look at a book, so she didn't," assured Lewis.

"I gotta put this back," Hemingway said, walking towards the truck. "You're lucky nothing happened!"

"Oh, yeah," muttered Lewis. "A portal to Hell opened, I beheaded a demon--- "

"Devil," corrected Shelly and Milton.

"Whatever. I got shot, almost died--- "Lewis said, emphasizing the sarcasm. "Yeah, this was **one big nothin'!**"

With the talent show over and the devil finally dispatched, the cousins headed for the Lodge. Shelly made an excuse to stop by Hem's place so that she could check on Lewis's bandage while Milton and Hemingway went back to the Lodge. The hunter had been letting her stay in the basement, which had once been a workshop for Hem's grandfather back in the 50s. It also had a sink and bathroom and became Shelly's makeshift apartment. A gadget in pieces on the workbench vaguely resembled a robot arm. Shelly was torn about lying to her cousin about the book.

49

"You live down here? In a workshop?"

"I kind of prefer it. Let's me work on projects. I'm pretty handy with tools. This used to belong to Hem's grandfather, I think."

Lewis noted all the tools that hung on the sheet of perforated wood. He touched what looked like some kind of vintage nail gun and got a vision.

He was standing in the basement, and an old hunter that vaguely resembled Hem, presumably his grandfather, was showing off the room to his four-year-old grandson. Four-year-old Hem was wearing a Piney Power hat and a t-shirt for the Mod Squad.

"Grandpa, I want hamburgers!" demanded young Hem.

"Of course you do," agreed his grandfather. "Your mother and her hippie shit. Feeding you twigs and grass! We'll go out and kill a deer. Make our own damned burgers."

"Yay!" laughed Hem, who picked up the nail gun. "Hunting!"

Hem's grandfather turned in his direction and got a horrified look on his face when he saw he held the nail gun.

"Now, Hemmy, that's not a toy. You put that down."

Hemingway fired off a nail, which bounced on the cement floor and shot across the room. The child laughed, finding it hilarious, and shot off two more, nearly impaling his grandfather's foot.

"Hey! You listen to me! You put that down!"

Hem fired another nail; this one caught his grandfather's sleeve and stuck him to the workbench.

"Hem! You listen to me, boy!"

But Hemingway, not realizing what he was doing, just kept laughing and pulling the trigger. Finally, one of the nails found itself in his grandfather's leg, and he started cursing a blue streak. Lewis came out of the vision.

"What the Hell?" muttered Lewis.

Shelly mistook Lewis' muttering for a complaint about the condition of the basement.
"I know. Everything had dust on it when I came down here, and the workbench is falling apart. Hem's not very handy," confessed Shelly.

"Yeah," agreed Lewis. "He doesn't seem the type that would be good with tools or building things. He's more like a destroyer."

"That's an accurate description."

"What kind of projects do you make? Like, uh, tire and rim stuff?"

"Nah, that's at work. Things like the crossbow. I'm working on a scope and this robot arm thing."

"You're building a robot?"

"No, just the arm. If I can get it to work, it can load one crossbow while I'm firing the other."

"You're a woman of many talents, I see."

"Yeah, right. I can't keep an apartment, a job, **and** learn to devil hunt. Hem lets me stay here. Never even asked me for rent."

"Wow, that's nice. Wish I had relatives like that."

"What's your family like?"

"It was just me and my dad, and he's gone, so…."

"Sorry."

"Eh. He smoked a lot. He was okay, I guess."

"No other family?"

"Nah. Not really."

"Kinda sad. I can't imagine my life without a dozen or so cousins getting into my business."

"Yeah, ya know. Orphan."

There was an awkward silence, then Shelly looked down and then blurted---

"I feel real bad about lying to Hem, Lewis," she said worriedly. "If we tell them now, it won't be as bad later."

"Look, we didn't technically lie," assured Lewis. "I'm the one that used the book, so anything bad that's going to happen is going to happen to me. Stop worrying."

"Yeah," Shelly said, telling herself it was fine. "I guess it doesn't matter as long as the devil's dead. Right?"

"Sure! That was the whole point, right?"

"How did you read the book?"

"I don't know. I just looked at it, and the words came out."

"Yeah, I mean, could you do that voice again?" she asked.

"What? Like…"

Lewis lowered his voice and mocked the words he had said earlier. The low rumbling of his voice turned Shelly on. It wasn't quite as good as before, but it was close enough. She knew they had time for another quickie before going back to the Lodge. Shelly kissed Lewis hard. They fell on Shelly's bed, hungrily kissing each other.

Unfortunately, back in the woods, the black dagger absorbed the rest of the devil's blood on its blade and began to transform. It morphed and grew into a man with a distinctly mid-90s suit and wide paisley tie. He adjusted his hair, smiled, and started walking towards the road.

In way of a non-apology, Hemingway had fired up the Lodge's grill and was making hamburgers for the cousins and their families. He wore a custom-made barbecue apron with the phrase "Curse the Cook" while twirling a pair of tongs and a barbecue spatula between his fingers. Several of the local wives came out with dishes of food. Whatever they had been cooking for dinner, they just packaged up and brought to the Lodge, creating an instant potluck.

Milton had struck up a conversation with Carol Simpkins, a 40-year-old divorcee with three wild kids, 6, 7, and 13, respectively. The three boys were running in and out of the Lodge with one of the mounted deer heads, pretending it was still alive, knocking over furniture, and bumping into the adults. Cousin Eliot stood next to the El Camino, talking to two other cousins about a potential repair and how the springloaded hood had performed earlier. Several of the cousins were playing cards, drinking, and arguing over topics local, national and international. Here and there, sullen teenagers were staring at their smartphones while a group of the older relatives played horseshoes and yelled at some of the children for running too close to the game. This was the expected level of chaos at a Galloway Family gathering.

Things were going great until Hemingway walked into the main lodge room with a tray of finished burgers stacked in a pyramid. He was ready to celebrate, but something he spotted suddenly darkened his mood. His hands went limp, and he dropped the entire tray in front of Byron and Wallace. A few burgers tumbled out of the pile and onto the floor.

"Something's wrong," said Hemingway, suddenly highly suspicious.

"What the Hell is wrong with you, Hem?" demanded Wallace, pulling the burger out of his lap.

"This is subpar for your apology barbecue," noted Byron. "Last time, you made rib tips."

"Cuz, are you okay?" asked Milton, looking away from Carol. "You got that look on your face, like when the Rain Man couldn't see Judge Wapner."

The secret passage, which was still partially opened to the back bar, had a row of devil heads with one missing. Hemingway marched over through a crowd of chaotic relatives.

"No," said Hemingway, aghast and disheartened.

Hem found the empty plaque on the floor.

"He's gone," said the hunter, holding up the plaque.

"Jesus, how did he notice that? I swear, Hem, you're autistic or something," added Byron.

"One of the heads is gone?" asked Milton. "No way it got off of here by itself."

"It's the Pussy Eater, Mil," said Hemingway grimly.

The room went dead silent. Lewis and Shelly walked in a few seconds later.

"Hey, what's goin' on?" asked Lewis. "What is this? A funeral?"

"You!" said Hemingway, picking up his barbecue fork like a weapon. "You!"

"Cuz, calm down," Shelly soothed.

"Did you know about this?!" demanded Hemingway.

There was confusion and even more chaos as the various cousins tried to talk over each other.

"What did you do?! What did you do?!" demanded Hem.

Milton held him back.

"Cuz, don't," he said sadly.

Lewis looked around, very worried the cousins might string him up.

"I used a book, okay? I had to! You said it was suicide to go in the sewer, and you both went in! What was I supposed to do? Huh?! You think I wanted to end up on the six o'clock news wanted for murder?!"

Feeling like he was being attacked, Lewis tried to back out of the room. Wallace shut the door and stood in his way.

"I told you not to touch the books!" screamed Hem, his face turning red.

"The devil's gone. Who cares?"

"How? How did you kill it?" asked Milton.

"I don't know. The spell or whatever made a dagger out of one of the devil heads."

Hemingway slapped the top of his forehead. The level of incompetence was draining him of energy and patience.

"I figured the devil could kill a devil, right? I mean, right?"

"You set loose the Pussy Eater," explained Byron.

Hemingway had calmed himself and looked like he was giving a quiet pep talk to Milton, who was staring wistfully ahead.

"What the Hell is that?"

"It was a level 25 plus Incubus. It was Milton's first big kill," explained Shelly quietly.

"So, he can kill it again, right?" asked Lewis hopefully.

"It killed his prom date on prom night," explained Shelly. "Not a good memory for him."

"Oh, Jesus, what did I do? I'm sorry, Milton," Lewis apologized.

Hemingway went for his fork again but instead threatened Eliot with it.

"And you gave him the book, Eliot!" shouted Hem.

"I pointed him to the Wallum Olum! I didn't think he could read it! No one could!"

"Leave him alone, Hem. He meant well," insisted Milton. "We gotta find him, and we gotta kill him. Tonight."

"Milton, he's got a head start on us, and we don't even know--
_ "

"Tonight!" insisted Milton. "Where did you see him, Lewis?"

"I-I-I didn't see anything," insisted Lewis. "After we killed the devil, that crazy portal opened up, and I lost the dagger in the woods."

"I'm gearing up," said Milton, striding out of the Lodge.

"Hem, I'm sorry," apologized Shelly, almost crying.

"You're in so much trouble, Shel', I don't even have time to yell at you," said Hemingway, searching on the Internet on his smartphone. "Here. Mil. Beauty pageant preliminaries in Wildwood. That sounds like ground zero for P.E. C'mon, fam!"

The Galloway hunters immediately stood and started heading out.

"Wait! Wait!" shouted Byron, stopping the exodus. "This entire situation has spiraled out of control thanks to **you**, Hemingway."

"Really, Byron? You're gonna measure dicks now?" snapped the hunter. "I'll measure mine, little man! Come at me, cuz!"

"Cuz, no offense, but you're not getting any younger," pointed out Byron. "You're a great hunter. My mentor. My **hero**."

"I'm sensing a 'but' here," Lewis muttered to Shelly.

"But this isn't cheeky teenager prodigy overreach. A powerful denizen of Hell is out there. He could kill a lot of people. He could kill some of us!"

"We're wasting time!" insisted Hem. "I helped Milton track down P.E. the first time!"

"We all were there," reminded Wallace. "It nearly killed you both. You gotta use some sense here, Hem."

"Milton is not thinking straight, and you know it!" insisted Byron. "The Eater's head has been up on the wall of the Lodge for years, thinking of a way to get revenge. Don't let this get further out of control!"

In the old days, Hemingway would've already been out the door. But something in Byron's words reached him. They had almost died on that hunt long ago. And even though Byron and Hemingway had their differences, they were still family, and family had to be trusted.

"All right, big man," Hem relented, smiling proudly at his protégé. "Make the call."

"Keep Milton here as long as you can, then keep him away from Wildwood. By the time he realizes his mistake, we'll take out the Eater," said Byron.

Hemingway looked away. He didn't like fooling Milton. There was no telling how mad he would get once he found out later.

"Okay. Be careful, cuz," said Hemingway, giving Byron a manly hug. "When you take him out, tell him Milton and Hemingway sent you."

"You be careful too," smiled Byron. "Don't break a hip."

"Shut up."

The Lodge cleared, leaving Shelly, Hem, and Lewis.

"Hey, man, I'm really sorry," said Lewis, apologizing to Hem.

Hem punched him in the gut, and Lewis fell in a heap.

"I guess I deserved that," gasped Lewis.

"C'mon, Hem," chastised Shelly. "Lee found his last name in the book; he could be family."

"Don't, Shel, just don't. Take this piece of shit, make sure he gets his stuff and gets out of town," instructed Hemingway.

The hunter marched out of the Lodge, wondering how he would keep Milton from going to Wildwood.

"C'mon, Lewis," said Shelly, helping the gambler to his feet. "You have to go."

As Lewis got to his feet, he reached up to keep his balance with one of the tables. On the table was the empty devil plaque. As he stood, his hand brushed against it, and another vision hit him.

Chapter 7

He saw the man with the paisley tie and the '90s haircut and knew instantly it was the Eater. It had walked out of the woods somewhere around Route 9. A dayshift waitress was heading home after work when she made the mistake of slowing down to ask the man if he needed help. He smiled at her, and something about him was so magnetic that she immediately let him in the car. Seconds later, strange noises came from the car as it shook. The man, having slid now to the driver's side, shoved a desiccated corpse with a tattered waitress uniform out of the driver's side door and drove off. A few minutes later, the waitress's car headed toward Atlantic City.

Lewis emerged from the vision, disoriented for a moment. Shelly had already walked him most of the way back to Hemingway's farm.

"Whoa, what happened?" muttered Lewis.

"You. You happened, Lewis," said Shelly, a little bitter. "This is what I get for falling for a guy who pays me a little attention. I get used."

"Shelly, it's not like that. I swear!" insisted Lewis. "I really like you. Like we have a connection."

"Stop it, Lewis!" demanded Shelly, letting go of his hand. "You used me to lie to my cousins!"

"I made a mistake! It was wrong! C'mon! Let me try and help!"

"You've done enough. Go inside and get your things. I'll go get your car."

"Listen to me, I saw something when I touched the plaque--- "

Shelly waved him off and went to get his car. Lewis made an exasperated noise and went back into Shelly's basement. Inside, he picked up the clothes he changed out of after he had sex with Shelly. Looking up, he noticed a huge pile of silver bullets.

"Few dozen of these ought to make me even with Pete," he thought. "It's not like they would miss them."

Lewis hesitated. There'd be no turning back if he stole the bullets, but what the Hell. They were kicking him out. He grabbed a backpack and started filling it with bullets. In the process, he realized that Hem had stuffed the Walum Olum into the same pack. He looked down at the book.

"If I knew what I was doing, I could make this right. Not screw it up like the rest of my life," he muttered.

"Lewis…Lewis?" said a familiar voice in his head. "You can! I can teach you!"

"Oh, shit."

"Yessssssss!" Aunt Christie said, talking to him from the grave. "Let me teach you! You have a gift, Lewis!"

"You don't seem exactly **trustworthy**, Grandma Munster."

"Oh, you can trust me! Lee's test hasn't come back, but we're blood! You're a Galloway! And if you can't trust blood, who can you trust?"

"That's a pretty big coincidence," replied Lewis skeptically. "I just happen to run out of gas right near here? C'mon."

"I may have played a small part in…luring you here," admitted the witch.

"Do you have any idea how you messed up my life?!" snapped Lewis. "You bitch!"

"Witch. And I had to. You have a great gift! I can help you! We Galloways help each other. That's what family's all about!"

"Yeah, I can see how much **you** value family," said Lewis sarcastically. "Your own son hates you."

"I wasn't exactly mother-of-the-year, but Hemingway is strong! Independent! Isn't that what parents want for their children?"

"Maybe. I guess. Sure."

"Isn't that what your father wanted for you?"

"Don't go there."

"Like you, I see glimpses of the past, present, and future. Your father loved you, but you never thought he was proud. You never could shake the disappointment from his eyes. What was it? Your failed singing career? Your pathetic attempt at sports? Or that you couldn't hold a relationship together?"

For a moment, Lewis was standing in his father's apartment. It smelled like old cigarettes, feet, and Lysol. His father was slumped in the same lime green easy chair in front of the T.V., as he had been for decades. Slowly, over the years, he had sunk further and further into that chair.

The sadness in his eyes haunted Lewis. Just once, he had wanted to surprise him with good news before he died.

"You're crossing some red lines, dead woman!"

"What are you going to do? Kill me? Ahahahaha!" cackled the witch.

"I'm not letting you out. I'm not stupid."

"No, I owe you. Helping you will embarrass Hemmy, which is more than enough payment! You'll be a hero. Aren't you tired of being a failure?"

Something in the witch's words struck Lewis deep. He needed that win. Any win.

"For the record, I'm doing this for Shelly. This book gotta spell that'll send the Pussy Eater back to Hell?"

"Of course."

"And you got any spells that let me cheat at cards?"

"I can tell you seventeen of them!"

Lewis dumped out the bullets and grabbed the book.

"Let's do this."

Lewis marched out of the room. A few seconds later, he came back and scooped the bullets back into the backpack.

"Just in case this don't work."

A few houses away, Hemingway rushed into his cousin's house. Milton was in the basement. He had built his own version of a dojo with incense burners, a framed movie poster of Lone Wolf and Cub, and places to hold his many swords. The martial artist sat in a lotus position in front of an ornate katana. He tried to meditate, but instead, he relived his 90's prom night.

Milton had been an outcast in high school, which is probably why he identified so much with his cousin. After his parents' divorce at six, his dad had moved out of Abe's Hat. Hemingway had become his de facto father figure over the years, showing him how to hunt even before the other Galloways thought he was an appropriate age.

That May night was warm, but Hem had sprung for a top-of-the-line tux for his cousin. It was a custom fit that breathed well, and Milton had planned to show off his legendary dance steps. He walked to the Galloway farm and found Hemingway in the barn where his mother had made him live. Seinfeld was blaring, and Aunt Christie was yelling out the back window towards the barn.

"Where is my money, Hem?!" demanded the graying witch. "You're six dollars short for the electric bill!"

"Are you serious?! You're interrupting Seinfeld for an electric bill?! This is a new episode!"

Hemingway was still moderately fit in those days, and the gray was only starting to appear on the very edges of his temples. His trusty bloodhound, Phaser, made an annoyed noise. The old dog was on his last legs, but Hemingway made sure he had every comfort. He had named him Phaser after his favorite Star Trek weapon and mostly to piss off his mother, who wanted to name the dog something more hippie-witchy like SageMoon or Cerebus.

Upon seeing Milton, Aunt Christie changed gears. She could be charming when she wanted to be.

"Oh, hello, Milton. Don't you look nice?" she smiled. "Don't mind, Hem. He's just being Hem."

Hemingway scoffed at her as she went back inside. Hemingway then turned to Milton and looked at him admiringly.

"Nice! I told you that tux place was sweet. My boy, Chris, took care of ya?"

"Yeah, I mentioned you."

"You got condoms, right?"

"Yeah," Milton said, a little embarrassed.

"Dude, you gotta have condoms. This is the big game! Just be good to the truck, okay? I left some blankets in the backseat in case the motel doesn't work out," added the hunter tossing him the keys. "Banging under the stars. You might sell her on that."

"I don't know if I even want to have sex yet," admitted Milton.

"No, trust me, you do," assured Hem.

Hemingway turned his back to his mother's house and peeled off five twenty-dollar bills in the teenager's hand.

"Here, take this. Take this," urged the Hunter. "Don't let your aunt see."

"Why don't you just give her the six dollars?"

"It's the principle of the thing! That six dollars is not even electricity I use!"

A second later, the power went off in the barn.

"Seriously?!" Hem yelled back toward the house. "What the Hell is wrong with you, ma?! Phaser needs light and heat!"

"You got money to give to your cousin, but not your bills, I see!"

"This is his prom night! Don't ruin it, you selfish witch!" screamed Hemingway.

Milton tried to hand some of the money back, but his cousin dismissed him, angrily gesturing to keep the money.

"Thanks, Hem. You going hunting, cuz?"

"I might as well," replied Hem, suddenly getting louder. "Since I don't have a T.V. or any lights where I **live**!"

"Get my six dollars!"

"I'll do that! While I'm doing that, why don't you throw yourself down the stairs and break your neck, ya old bat!"

"Shut up!"

"I hope you do! And I hope you suffer while I'm trying to break a twenty so you can have **six dollars** for a bill you can't even pay until **Monday**!"

Milton started to leave in mid-argument. Hem gestured for him to come back, and he stopped.

"One more thing," added his cousin.

Hem grabbed Milton's arm and started pushing in various spots. Finally, he found the button on the cuff and turned it. An eight-inch blade slid out from the sleeve above Milton's hand.

"Jesus, Hem! What the Hell is that for?" said Milton in shock.

"Prepare for any eventuality, cuz," repeated Hem, incredulous, as if this was basic information everyone should know.

Milton turned the button and retracted the blade.

"I thought the arm was a little stiff. You might've warned me. What if this goes off when I'm having sex with Denise?"

"Most people take their clothes off, Milton."

"Yeah, but what if I didn't."

"It'll be fine; just laugh it off."

"What if I stab her by accident?"

"You're not going to have the jacket on when you bang her, all right?" said Hem impatiently. "Trust me, it's fine. Now, will you go?"

Milton remembered driving over to Denise's house. It was a magical hour from when he arrived and had his picture taken with Denise in front of her parents. When Denise's dad told him to take care of his daughter, he felt like a man for the first time. Responsible. Honest. Reliable. Not like his dad, who had left him.

The ride to the high school was just as magical. They talked and laughed, and Milton remembered imagining what Denise would be like as a mom. They had only been dating for a few weeks, but they had clicked effortlessly. He figured she knew that they'd be together always.

But he would never get to know for sure.

They had gotten to the prom a little late, and most of the parking spots were taken. Milton was still a little unsure driving Hem's pickup, so he parked far in the back of the lot. The Cure's "Friday, I'm in Love" played from the gym. When they got out of the truck, they kissed, and almost immediately, Milton felt the presence of another person standing nearby.

"Hey, buuu-uuuddy."

Milton and Denise both simultaneously turned toward the voice. He was a strikingly handsome kid with piercing blue eyes.

"Can I help you?" asked Milton, not recognizing him.

"Kind of a dark parking lot. Be happy to escort your girl inside while you check out that oil leak in your truck."

There was something so confident and sure about the way he said it that, for a moment, Milton was going to take him at his word.

But he checked himself and questioned this supposed authority just like his cousin did with almost anyone that challenged him.

"It's fine," he assured Denise, an orange glow flickering behind the strange kid's eyes.

Denise was instantly mesmerized and took a few steps forward as the handsome man offered his hand. Milton realized he was dealing with one of the devil spawn.

"Oh, shit," Milton muttered, fumbling for the cuff.

As Denise turned away, the man backhanded Milton and hurled him against a nearby car. His date seemed not to notice. On the ground, Milton extended the blade, scrambled to his feet, and charged. The arrogant creature, not expecting a weapon or someone who knew how to use it, turned too slowly. Milton slashed his back open, and the devil howled.

This time, it backhanded Milton over the fence at the edge of the parking lot. Milton landed on the grass of the football field, his blade snapping from the impact. Denise snapped out of her daze for a split second, but the creature grabbed her by the neck and lifted her off the ground.

"Milton?! What's happening?" she choked.

Milton picked up his broken blade and rushed to scramble over the fence, but he was too late. The devil's face opened up to reveal a horrifying maul of teeth and tentacles. Denise was screaming his name.

"Milton?" called Hemingway skidding to the edge of the doorway and snapping him out of his flashback.

"Shoes!" Milton demanded, without even looking up.

Hemingway rolled his eyes and hastily stripped off his sneakers. He took a half step into the room.

"Bow!" insisted Milton.

Usually, Hemingway would flaunt these kinds of requests, but he was in a hurry and in no mood for his cousin to kick his ass Bushido-style.

"Listen to me, Milton, please," pleaded Hemingway. "You're not in a good frame of mind for this."

"That's why I'm meditating," replied his cousin, eyes still shut. "When I achieve the balance, we'll go."

"Milton, this isn't a good--- "

62

"We'll **go**," Milton said more insistently. "Don't make this harder than it is, Hem!"

Hemingway wasn't confident in his lying abilities. If this didn't work, maybe he could calm his cousin down enough so he could fight with a clear head. He had to play to his strengths, so he did something totally uncalled for.

"Lone Wolf and Cub. Remember when I took you to that?"

Milton kept his eyes closed but smiled despite himself. "Yes. I loved it."

"Did I buy you the comic book?"

"Yeah. It's upstairs. I keep it by my bed."

There was an awkward pause.

"You don't…do stuff to yourself with the book, right?"

"What? No! What the Hell are you asking?" said Milton, opening an eye.

"It just sounded weird. Most of the stuff near my bed is porn, so…."

"You still have paper porn?"

"Paper, digital, live-action--- It's all good."

"Okay," said Milton, giving up the ghost. "Let's go; I have to end this conversation."

Milton stood up and grabbed the sword.

"Listen, I told the other cousins I would try to keep you from going to Atlantic City," admitted Hem sheepishly.

"You said P.E. is in Wildwood," Milton corrected suspiciously.

"I lied. You gotta bust me in the chops, so they know I tried, okay?"

Milton popped him, but Hem just shrugged it off.

"No, harder. Leave a mark."

"There is a mark."

"It's not enough, I can tell."

"It's your face. You can't even see it!"

"Exactly my point!"

Milton popped him again. This time Hem staggered backward into the wall, nearly pulling down the Lone Wolf and Cub poster. He recovered and looked at himself in the reflection of the glass.

"Once more."

"Jesus, Hem! What do you want me to do? Beat the crap out of you?"

"You're pulling your punch, I can tell!"

"I don't want to hurt you!"

"I just want it to be convincing!"

"Fine!"

This time, Milton took a good stance, feigned in the opposite direction to let Hem drop his guard, and then struck him; the hunter lifted up and landed hard on the dojo floor.

"Oh, God," he gasped in pain. "Too hard."

"Dammit, c'mon. Let's get to A.C. then."

As Milton helped Hem to his feet, the hunter smiled, pleased that he had sold such a big lie.

Outside, Shelly made eye contact with Lewis as his jeep rolled down the street. There was nothing else for her to say. Hem and Milton came outside, and Milton handed off Hem to Shelly.

"Here, Shel," said Milton. "I'll get the truck."

"I'm driving!" insisted Hemingway.

"Only if you're standing on your own when I come back," insisted Milton.

When Milton got out of earshot, Hem instantly recovered.

"We're going to A.C., intern," Hem informed her.

"You actually convinced him? Milton's going to beat the crap out of you when he finds out."

"Yeah, he's halfway there. Get the gear and lots of bullets. This has got to look like the real thing to him."

Shelly rushed inside her workshop. She grabbed various weapons, a backpack full of bullets and guns, and another with a bright orange X on the back. On the way out of the door, she spotted another pack that looked like the one Hem had used to hold the Wallum Olum. She immediately realized what had happened.

Running back outside, she held the empty bag so Hem could see.

"No! No-no-no-no!" the hunter said. "That sonuvabitch took it!"

"Lewis took the book?" said Milton, incredulous. "Why? He couldn't use it the first time."

"Because he's a thief and a liar," concluded Shelly, sadly.

Hem looked toward his mother's grave in the backyard. In the great distance, he could hear her cackle.

"Oh, no! You are not doing this to me, you old witch!" insisted the hunter.

Furious, Hemingway marched into the backyard, picked up the nearest shovel, and started digging.

"Where is he?! You tell us where he took that book, ma!"

Milton and Shelly rushed to the graveside.

"Hem, we got bigger fish to fry, man!" insisted Milton.

"Lewis already summoned P.E. by himself! Think of what he could do with ma's help!" insisted the hunter. "Now you tell me, you old broad! Or I swear to God I will drag your rotten corpse out to the crematorium right now!"

Aunt Christie cackled just beneath the mound of dirt.

"That's it; I don't have time for this," said Milton throwing up his hands.

"Shelly, don't let him leave without us!" insisted Hem.

"I'm not leaving without you," said Milton, going inside Hem's house.

A minute later, Milton came outside with a tray full of various Hummel figurines.

"Hem, throw down that shovel. Now," threatened Milton.

"Hey! Those Hummels are worth money!" insisted Hemingway. "Get them back inside before you break them!"

"My Hummels?! You have my Hummels?" said the witch. "I spent years collecting them!"

"Yeah, and you're going to spend years trying to pick up the pieces unless you tell Hem where Lewis went with the book!" threatened Milton.

Milton then shook his head silently, assuring Hemingway he was just bluffing.

"What's it going to be, Aunt Christie?"

"All right! All right!" said the witch, relenting. "He's going to Atlantic City, but good luck finding him!"

Milton turned back into the house to put the Hummels back but misjudged the width of the doorway. The tray hit the side of the door jam, flipping the tray and dropping the Hummels all over the ground. The fragile figurines broke against the brick pathway just outside the door. Hemingway mouthed the word, "Fuck!" over and over again.

"What was that?" asked Aunt Christie.

"Uh, I dropped my keys!" Hemingway said immediately. "Go back to sleep, ma!"

Hemingway gestured for his cousins to get into the truck. Milton tossed the tray aside and climbed into the pickup with Shelly. Hemingway got behind the wheel, started it up, jammed it in gear, and peeled out all over the driveway. The gravel rained down on his mother's grave.

Just below the dirt, Christie's rotten eyes rolled back into her head and started to glow a bright green.

"Lewis," she said in an otherworldly voice that traversed the distance and emanated from the book. "To get to Atlantic City faster, use the spell on page six."

Lewis had just gotten on the Expressway. He pulled the Walum Olum out, counted the pages, and looked at the various symbols.

"How do I use the--- "

Before he could finish the sentence, the book seemed to possess him again. Lewis began speaking in the 12,000-year-old language while he rolled past billboards for the various casinos. Two shadowy demons materialized on either side of the jeep, grabbed the car's sides, and pushed it down the highway. It rocketed down the Expressway at breakneck speed.

"The fuck?!" said Lewis, holding onto the steering wheel for dear life.

"Speed demons!" cackled Aunt Christie in way of explanation.

Within minutes, Lewis had skidded to a halt in front of the newly built Poolside Resort and Casino. His jeep began to sputter. The fast travel had taken its toll on the jeep. The care Lewis had lavished on the vehicle to keep it on the road faded; rust spots and dents were everywhere. Even the seats and the top became cracked and worn.

"What the Hell did you do to my jeep?!" demanded Lewis.

"There was a price. The devils always take their price!" cackled the witch.

66

"Whatever, let's find this guy."

"Devil."

"Whatever! Where do I go?"

"You could use a page in the book--- "

"No, I don't need my eyeballs rolling out of my head before I confront him! Where would he be?"

"Wherever the beautiful ladies go."

Lewis looked around. Almost immediately, an electronic billboard lit up announcing the "Strip Off" at the Poolside.

"Wait, did you use the spell?"

"No."

"So a billboard holding the exact information I need immediately lights up in front of me? Seems convenient."

"When you deal with the occult and magic, that kind of thing always happens. It's the synchronicity of the world!"

"Oh, boy, you really were a hippie," said Lewis dismissively.

Chapter 8

Somewhere outside of Abe's Hat, Hemingway was taking a shortcut through the woods in his truck. The truck went airborne at an intersection with a blinking yellow light, scraping the top of the truck's roof before roughly landing and moving on. Shelly checked her seatbelt for the fifth time to make sure it was secure.

"Hem! Get us there in one piece, huh?!" shouted Milton, trying to steady himself with the roof handle.

"Please," scoffed Hem. "I've been driving these back wood roads since I was ten. Besides, Shelly installed the deer thing."

"I did?"

"The what?"

"The deer thing! You know. Makes the deer avoid me."

"You mean a deer whistle?" asked Shelly.

"Yes!" insisted Hem impatiently.

"I never installed that."

"Are you sure? I could've sworn--- "

Distracted, it was at that moment a deer ran out onto the road. Hem swerved and ended up stopping in a roadside ditch.

"Dammit! C'mon! We gotta get to Lewis!" cursed Hem, getting out of the truck.

"Uh, hello, P.E.," reminded Milton.

"Yeah, Lewis is just a distraction at this point," agreed Hem, casting a guilty glance toward Shelly.

Hem checked the truck.

"Well, looks like no broken axel this time," he announced.

"It's so weird," mocked Shelly. "And you've been driving in these woods since you were ten."

"No one likes a mouthy intern," reminded Hem.

Milton got a faraway look in his eye.

"What? What is it?" said his cousin impatiently.

"Maybe I can't do this," said Milton, unsure of himself. "That night at the prom--- Denise needed me and--- "

"No! Do not do that!" insisted Hem. "You were only eighteen!"

"You were **sixteen** when you beat Todd!"

Hem looked at Shelly, unsure of what to say. He'd been telling that story for as long as he could remember. In the past, it had served him; now, it was screwing with Milton's head.

"I was **on** that day," explained Hem. "Everything that could've gone right went right. And I've never been able to repeat it. Not even close. My entire life is built around that moment. I'm like one of those guys who peaked in high school."

Hem dropped his arms, realizing what he had just said.

"Oh-my-God-I-peaked-in-high-school," Hem realized to his horror.

"But Milton," said Shelly, taking over the pep talk. "You're not like that, and what happened to you was just unlucky. You were in the middle of going to prom; Hem wasn't doing anything. He had nothing else going on in his life."

"Hey!" objected Hem. "What she's trying to say is, I had everything going for me that day. It was broad daylight, we were getting ready for a softball game, I already had the bat--- Todd was after the other cousins; he never saw me coming until I kneecapped him. And he was a big, dumb devil spawn. P.E. is cunning. He would've eaten me alive, but not you. You survived, and we hunted that asshole down, and you killed him!"

He lifted Milton's head up.

"You're a hunter. You're a Galloway. The hunt is your world! You own it, cuz!" insisted Hem.

Shelly heard something moving in the woods nearby.

"Guys..." she started to warn.

"Hem, you were right about my relationships--- "

"I was just shooting my mouth off. Ignore me."

"No, it's true. Since Denise, I never wanted a relationship that was any good. I don't think I deserve them. I'm not worthy. I can't protect them."

"You can!" insisted Hem.

Shelly could hear something, and it sounded like it was rushing closer to their position.

"Guys!" she insisted.

"Give us a moment, Shel! He's having an existential crisis!"

Suddenly, the desiccated husk of the waitress came lunging out of the darkness. The shriveled corpse was still wearing the uniform, and its eyes were glowing embers of orange. It screeched and charged right at Hemingway's back. Milton pushed him aside and, with a flourish of his sword, cut the creature's arms and head off. It collapsed into ash in front of him.

"That's why I don't give myself over to a relationship," continued Milton, like the monster never appeared.

Hemingway and Shelly couldn't believe Milton was still whining. Hemingway held up his hands with a stunned expression on his face.

"Dude, you know the divorce rate amongst hunters in the Lodge," his cousin reminded him. "The manliness brings in the ladies, but the Hunt drives them away."

"What Hem is saying," interpreted Shelly. "You're gonna find someone. The fact that you're saying all this means you know the problem. Right?"

"Yeah," said Milton, finally coming out of his daze. "I do. Let's go solve that problem."

"Now that's what I'm talking about!" said Hemingway, excited. "Let's go cut P.E.'s dick off and feed it to him!"

"Dial it back, Hem," warned Milton.

"There's my cousin killjoy," replied Hem

The cousins got back in the truck and sped towards A.C.

Lewis was making his way toward the Strip Off. He spotted a side entrance from the self-park parking lot and headed for it. Flipping through the Walum Olum, he stopped at the page the witch instructed him to use.

"So this is going to send the demon--- "

"Devil."

"**Devil** back to Hell?"

"Yes," assured the witch.

Lewis looked at the page. He could hear the words in his head and muttered them softly.

"Stop! Stop!" warned Aunt Christie. "You have to see the devil to make it work."

"All right, all right," said Lewis, stopping. "Just getting warmed up."

As Lewis walked with his head in the book, Pete had been sneaking up on him. Besides Lewis not showing up for his poker tournament, the loan shark had discovered a slow leak in his back passenger tire. He had just finished putting on the donut when he spotted Lewis making his way toward the casino entrance. He caught up to him with a few wide strides and clobbered him with the tire iron. Lewis went down, and the Walum Olum flipped shut, cutting off a surprised noise from the witch that Pete didn't hear. The synchronicity of the world could work against you as well.

"This is why you return calls," Pete explained with an angry hand gesture to the unconscious Lewis.

On the streets of A.C., Hem had pulled into a spot a block away from the casinos.

"Gimme the goggles," requested Hem.

"You brought the goggles?" said Milton, a little incredulous. "You told me the goggles didn't work so well."

"It's an ongoing project," assured Hem. "Right, intern?"

"If you mean ongoing that you can put them on your face, then yeah," said Shelly, unsure. "Please don't shoot anyone with the goggles on."

"You made the lenses with silver flakes, the battery puts a charge in them, and you can see devils and their ilk," assured the hunter, strapping on the goggles.

"Didn't you shoot all the air conditioning units in the bowling alley chasing a Level 9 Blood Drinker?" reminded Milton.

"Like I said, ongoing project. It's just that the cold air coming out of air conditioning units looks a lot like devil magic through these."

"Seems like a big drawback," muttered Milton.

"Shut up, please," said Hem.

The hunter turned on the goggles. The thousands of air conditioning units covering Atlantic City's hotels, motels, shopping malls, and casinos lit up the street like a Christmas tree inside the goggles.

"Shit," muttered Hem.

The cousins started walking to the casino. Hem bumped into a telephone pole and kept smacking the goggles hoping they would suddenly work. An electric shock ripped through them for a second, stinging his face.

"Ow! Goddammit!"

"Hem! Will you take those off?!" insisted Milton.

Hem spotted a large glowing object on the street around the next corner.

"No-no-no, I got something," he insisted.

Hem rushed to the corner of a building, and Shelly guided him away from walking straight into the wall. Parked a few spaces away near that corner was Lewis's jeep.

"What is it? I can't see it," said Hem shielding his eyes from its bright glow.

"It looks like Lewis's jeep," said Shelly. "But older."

Frustrated, Milton pulled the goggles off of Hem's face and let them snap onto his forehead.

"We don't have time for this," said Milton impatiently. "The Pussy Eater has killed God-knows-how-many women by now."

"I know, cuz, but we gotta get Lewis while he's here," insisted Hem. "Who knows what he's going to unleash with that book unsupervised."

"You two go save him," said Milton walking toward the Strip Off sign. "I'm on the hunt."

"You can't take P.E. on yourself," insisted Shelly.

"Watch me, cuz," dared Milton.

Hem stopped Shelly from walking after Milton.

"We're good. Let him spin his wheels while we go find your boyfriend," said Hem.

"What?" said Shelly, suddenly worried. "Why did you call him that?"

"Nothing, I was just screwing around. What?"

"What?"

"Nothing."

"Okay."

"Fine!"

"Okay!"

"Are we talking about the same thing?" asked Hem, confused.

"Yes," said Shelly carefully, as if stepping over a land mine. "Maybe I can adjust the goggles when you have them on."

"Good idea."

Hem turned around, and Shelly took out a small screwdriver to adjust the flow of the electricity through the lenses.

"Ow-ow-ow!" said the hunter. "Starting to sting my face!"

Shelly adjusted the screw the other way, and the world came into focus. Hem could see Pete's car a block away, and a bright glow on the passenger seat came from the Walum Olum.

"I got the book! It's in that car! C'mon, intern!"

Hem walked straight into a stop sign, changed gears, and headed for the truck.

Several minutes later, Pete had driven Lewis to an abandoned rowhouse scheduled for demolition. He had the Walum Olum on a table and Lewis tied to a chair. He found a cup of filthy water left behind from the last tenant and splashed Lewis in the face with it.

"Ah! What was that?!" demanded Lewis.

"Piss and rainwater, probably," said Pete slipping on some black leather gloves.

"Whoa-whoa-whoa, Pete! You gotta hold on here! I can get your money!" insisted Lewis.

"Oh, yeah," said Pete, feigning interest. "How you gonna do that with your arms and legs broken?"

"Look-look, in my pockets! I got silver! Take it!"

Pete searched Lewis's pockets and found the bullets.

"Silver bullets? What are you? The Lone Ranger? Do I look like Tonto to you? Where'd you even get these?"

"It's a long story, but they're real; take 'em. Give me some time to get the rest."

"What am I supposed to do with these, idiot? Melt them down? This is not how I like to be paid. What about this book, huh? This worth anything?"

"That? No, don't mess with that."

"Don't **mess** with a **book**. What is a librarian going to **get** me?" said Pete, incredulous. "How's a book gonna hurt me?"

"The book has got powers, and I can use them to--- "

Pete started laughing despite himself.

"Powers? Are you Spiderman?" laughed the gangster.

"Seriously! It's a spellbook! I got spells so I can run the tables!" insisted Lewis. "Just let me show it to you!"

"Are you shittin' me? You finally cracked Lewis."

"I know what it sounds like, but trust me--- "

"Trust you? Now **that's** funny," Pete laughed. "Let's see what's got you so spooked."

Pete flipped through the Walum Olum, but the symbols and pictures meant nothing to him.

"What is this?" he said, confused.

"You can't read it," Lewis explained, frustrated. "It's written in a 12,000-year-old language that no one understands."

"But **you** can?" said Pete skeptically. "I didn't think you could read a whole book in English! Aren't you the guy that had to take his G.E.D, **twice**?"

"I know," said Lewis, resigned. "If you just met my cousins, they could explain."

"Yeah, well, there's been a management shake-up with some of **my** cousins," Pete explained, tossing the open book aside.

Pete withdrew a Glock from a holster under his sports jacket.

"I've been told to close all outstanding accounts," Pete explained. "Nothin' personal. I honestly would've loved to have watched you try and use that thing to get my money, but I'm on the clock."

"No-no-no!" Lewis begged, trying to think of something to stop Pete.

It was at that moment, the door was kicked in. Atlantic City's finest had arrived to save the day, much to Lewis's relief. There were four officers in tactical armor and one plainclothes female detective in a Kevlar vest.

"Freeze! Drop the gun!"

Pete immediately relented. He dropped the gun and put up his hands, more annoyed than anything.

The detective frisked Pete as she talked. She was in her 50's but was fit. She had an old-style, 80's hairdo and a jaded look on her face.

"Hey, Pete," she greeted. "We've been looking for you."

"Detective Galloway, we were just rehearsing a play," said Pete flatly.

Lewis looked up at the mention of the detective's name. One of the other cops untied him.

"Really? With a real loaded gun? Guess you're committed to your craft, huh?" said Detective Galloway. "Don't worry, you're gonna have plenty of downtime in Rahway."

Detective Galloway threw Pete down against the table, and he fell face-first into the Walum Olum. Magical energies burned his face for a moment, and the images from the book made their way onto his face and then faded. For a second, his eyes glowed orange. Pete's expression changed to one of fear. He didn't understand what happened, but he knew something weird was going on.

"What the fuck was that?" demanded Pete, who turned to Lewis. "What was that?! What the Hell did you do?!"

Galloway shoved Pete toward the other officers and picked up the book.

"Take him out of here. I'll take the victim to my car," Galloway instructed.

"This ain't over, Lewis!" shouted Pete. "When I get out, you better hide! I will find you!"

The other cops dragged Pete out of the room.

"Can I ask you something?" Lewis began.

"Let's get you outside first, sir," assured the detective. "You and your antique book are safe."

Galloway closed the book and shoved it under Lewis's jacket. She looked into his eyes, ensuring the instructions were clear to him.

"We need to get you outside, **cuz,**" she said in a lower voice so the other officers wouldn't hear.

74

Lewis quickly found himself ushered out a side entrance, away from the other cops. In an alley near the abandoned rowhome, Hem and Shelly were waiting.

"Hem! Shel!" said Lewis in relief. "You saved me!"

"Technically, the ACPD did," corrected the detective. "Do I even want to know what this is all about?"

"Probably not," admitted Hem. "Lewis, this is Darla, my ex-wife. Still sexy and fine as ever."

"Your game's so rusty it squeaks, Hem," said Darla, smiling despite herself.

"I'll take it from here," assured Hem.

Hem tossed Lewis into a nearby set of trashcans and began beating him.

"Hem! No! Stop!" Shelly begged.

"Just a few more minutes," he assured. "I haven't heard that crack."

Darla pulled Hem off Lewis, who let his arms fall limply at his side.

"What the Hell, Darla?!" snapped Hem.

"I didn't do you a favor so you could kill 'em!"

"Oh, I've killed lots of people," assured Hem.

"Not the non-possessed ones; you haven't!"

"He stole a book, Darla! And you know how I feel about books!"

The Walum Olum fell out of Lewis's jacket, and Shelly picked it up.

"I was tryin' to help, I swear," said Lewis breathlessly.

"Seriously, when you guys are on a hunt, you're supposed to call ahead," reminded Darla.

"There was no time," insisted Hem. "And after I saved the mayor, I think we're owed a little leeway."

"That was **two** mayors ago," reminded Darla. "I told you before, you can't let stuff like this go public. People will go nuts."

"The Pussy Eater got loose," explained Shelly. "But we think he's in Wildwood."

"No, he's not!" insisted Lewis. "That's why I came here!"

"Shut up, Lewis," said Hem threateningly. "Haven't you done enough damage? I should pull your eyes through your mouth!"

"What does that mean?" asked Darla, confused.

"I don't know! I'm angry!" added Hem.

"I'm serious. I can see things. Like your mother could," said Lewis. "She showed me how to use it a little."

"Prove it," said Hem skeptically. "Darla, you still got the ring?"

Darla rolled her eyes, reached under her vest, and pulled out the end of a necklace with a class ring on the end of it. Hem pointed to it.

"Touch it," dared the hunter.

Lewis grabbed the ring. Instantly he saw an image of a 16-year-old Hemingway and his high school girlfriend, Darla, under the bleachers at Abe's Hat High. Hem was completely bloody, having just beaten to death a devil using various pieces of sporting equipment. Hem bent down on one knee, took off his class ring, wiped the blood off, and slid it on Darla's finger.

"To Hell and back, baby," said Hem trying to be suave. "That's how I do."

Lewis came out of the vision.

"To Hell and back, baby, that's how I do?" he repeated, incredulous. "What does that even mean?"

Hem got annoyed and ripped the ring out of Lewis's hand.

"I had just saved her from a Level 6 Teeth Smasher, using nothing but the stuff from the sports equipment shed!" said Hem, a bit outraged. "You people know **nothing** of romance!"

"I think it was more that you saved my life," corrected Darla, taking the necklace back. "I didn't even remember what you said. Just that, uh, you were pretty hot back in your prime."

"I never left my prime, baby," assured Hem. "I'm one hundred percent prime beef, all day and all night."

"Please stop," said Shelly, trying to focus the group. "If Lewis can see the visions, then did you see--- "

"Yes! The Pussy Eater changed course. He was going to Wildwood until he saw a billboard for the Strip Off! He's **here**!"

"Oh, shit! Milton's hunting him alone!" realized Hem.

Chapter 9

Milton walked through a nightclub at the Poolside Resort and Casino called Reflections. Some of A.C.'s hottest ladies were dancing the night away. There was a long bar with neon trim and top-shelf liquor while bartenders plied their trade to the young, hip gambling populace. Milton seemed severely underdressed for the room, but he stuck to the darker side of the club, which he had slipped inside while someone was coming out.

Reflections was a hunter's nightmare. There was too much noise, light, and people. With all the distractions, Milton tried to shut it all out. He sat at the bar in front of someone else's abandoned drink. Underneath the din, he could make out the faint sound of sinister whispers.

Across the room, he spotted him. P.E. had changed his clothes. He wore a modern suit with an open collar and even updated his hairstyle. Laughing and drinking with some of the strippers, they all seemed to be having a good time. Then, he dismissed himself and headed for the restroom. Milton followed, hyperfocused on his prey.

He found him at a urinal inside the bathroom, pretending to take a piss. There was no one else inside. Milton locked the door and drew a hilt. A blade collapsed out of it, unfolding into a perfect silver katana.

"Hey, bu-udddy," said P.E. "No since pretending, right? You know I'm not peeing. Devils don't need to pee. Although, sometimes, we like to do it in Hell. We'll pee on the damned just for a laugh. You gotta keep morale up somehow, right?"

"You're not leaving this bathroom in one piece," threatened Milton.

"Maybe," admitted the fiend. "You're a lot better hunter than when we met. All the years I spent as a mounted head on the wall watching you. Waiting. I think it matters to Denise if you send me back to Hell."

"Don't you say her name!"

"She's still inside me, Milton. I ate her **soul**," explained the devil. "Help me, Milton! Please! Help me!"

The last part, P.E. said in Denise's voice.

"Stop it," ordered Milton. "I'm going to rip you to pieces for you what you did. And I'm going to move your head to the bottom of a urinal in the lodge."

"That's not me doing her voice; that's **her**," said the devil innocently. "She's inside me. Her soul tasted...sweet."

"You don't know her. You're just trying to make me do something stupid out of anger," said Milton flatly. "It won't work."

"I do know. I know everything about her," said the fiend. "She was in love with you. Totally willing to give herself to you. Body and soul. But the body is dead, and the soul is mine."

Milton lunged, swinging the sword, but P.E. was unnaturally fast. After a few swings, all Milton had managed to accomplish was to severely damage the stalls.

"You're gonna die, Milton," explained the devil. "Even if you get me today and live to a ripe old age. And whether I'm in the urinal at the hunting club, running around loose or back in Hell, I'm just gonna keep eating souls. After a thousand years, do you think anyone will remember you? Your cousins? Your silly lodge? Even then, Denise will still be trapped inside me. All you're doing by hunting me is hurting her."

"You're lying!" insisted Milton. "You're just trying to distract me with her voice."

"He's not lying, Milton!" P.E. said in Denise's voice again. "Just leave him alone! You can't kill him! You can't free us!"

Milton lunged again, but P.E. was ready. He used his forward momentum to send him sailing into a toilet. The devil moved to kick down the locked door, but as he lifted his foot, Milton whipped out a throwing star. It struck the creature right in his Achilles tendon (or what would've been if he were human) and collapsed under the weight. This gave Milton time to stand up, and as soon as he did, the devil and he were in a stand-off again.

"That hurt," said the fiend. "But we devils are used to pain. In a thousand years, who will care? There was a Sumerian like you. Had a tribe of warriors that hunted us like your cousins. I ate the souls of his wife and daughters. He sent me back to Hell, but who remembers him? I still have their souls. I still **exist**. He's dust. A forgotten ghost. Feel small yet? See where this is going?"

Back on the streets, Hem's truck and Darla's car skidded to a halt in front of the Poolside. The group got out of their respective vehicles.

"I can't believe you're still driving that thing," said Darla as Hem got out.

"I don't remember you complaining back in the day. You up for this hunt?" asked Hem.

"I think I got a few silver bullets left," she said, sounding game.

The hunter turned and suddenly held Darla by the waist.

"How 'bout a little sugar for the road?" he asked mischievously.

"Um, how about I have a **boyfriend?**" said Darla, mildly indignant.

Hem stared through her, not believing.

"You don't, do you?" Hem smiled roguishly.

Darla sighed and looked away.

"No," she admitted. "Fine."

The couple kissed while Shelly and Lewis, who had rushed toward the front door of the Poolside, now came running back.

"Seriously?" said Lewis.

"Lotta history here," explained Hem, waving a finger between him and Darla. "And the sexual tension is off the charts. Why do you think we got married?"

"Uh, because you wanted to move out of your mother's place," suggested Darla. "And I didn't want to live in a barn."

"Baby, you know my rule," said Hem. "Let's not fight until after the sex is over."

"You guys can have old people sex later," insisted Shelly, mildly disgusted. "Let's go find Milton, please?"

"Aw! That was uncalled for, intern," said the hunter, following the group toward the casino.

"I resent that remark," added Darla.

"I hope to resemble that remark later," added Hem, slapping Darla on the butt.

Inside Reflections, Milton and P.E.'s battle had spilled out into the bar. The devil had hurled Milton against the bathroom door, ripping it off its hinges. Milton slid backward into the bar, smacking the stools so hard against it that it cracked the finish. His katana had skittered somewhere off into the darkness.

P.E. came charging out of the room as Milton regained his feet with one quick kung-fu style leap. Dancers and bar-goers were running all over the room, trying to get out of the way. The devil grabbed the nearest dancer and held her fast. She screamed in surprise.

"How about this one, Milton? Can you live with her death on your hands? Just walk out of here," offered the devil.

"We both know I'm not that stupid," said Milton, glancing around for the katana.

P.E. got the message and let the girl go.

"Looking for something?" smiled the creature.

The Eater lunged forward, but Milton had been playing him. He had dug out and repaired the old blade Hem had given him on prom night. It slid from Milton's sleeve as the creature charged. Milton caught the beast under the chin and across the face, sending him reeling into some seats.

"Damn," it said in a much more gravelly voice. "I guess **I'm** that stupid."

The devil's eyes began to glow, and its fingernails started to elongate into sharpened points. But the Poolside security team arrived, and P.E. immediately shifted gears. Their uniforms were khaki shorts and polo shirts with the casino logo, but they aimed brand new tasers at Milton. The demonic glow faded from P.E.'s eyes, his fingernails returned to normal, and he was now an injured, bleeding man who'd been assaulted.

"Drop the sword!" insisted the security guards.

"Help me! Oh, God! I need a hospital!" moaned P.E.

"Don't let him leave!" shouted Milton, dropping the sword and putting his hands behind his head.

The Pussy Eater immediately moved toward the only female in the squad.

"Please! Help me!" begged the fiend. "I think he severed a tendon in my jaw!"

"It's okay, sir," said the young woman. "Let me see."

"No, don't look in his eyes!" screamed Milton.

Milton took a step forward, and one of the guards tasered him. He fell to one knee. Behind the bulk of the guards, the face of the

80

Pussy Eater peeled back, the layers of skin on its face opening like some weird limp octopus. Underneath was a demonic skull and a round mouth full of jagged teeth. It opened immediately, and the lady security guard's soul began to be pulled from her body. Almost immediately, her body started to collapse in on itself.

Although the electric shock made it hard to move, Milton used his sleeve as an insulator and pulled the barbed taser hooks out of his torso. He hurled them back at the guard who shot him, and the brief shock caused him to drop the weapon. Another guard immediately followed up with another shot, but Milton blocked the barbs with a barstool and pointed at the horror behind them.

"Look!" he shouted.

The guard that had shot him turned. He was so rattled and thinking of two expressions of surprise simultaneously, he only managed to scream, "Oh, my shit!" The other guards turned, and their fellow guard was being quickly drained of her life force.

"No-no-no!" shouted Milton.

He threw the bar stool aside, picked up the blade he had dropped, and hurled it at the devil. It struck the fiend in the arm, and he let go of the security guard, but it was too late. He had already eaten her soul. The partially drained husk of a woman with sunken eyes staggered and growled. It was now some mindless undead beast with gray skin and white wisps of hair.

The Eater's face returned to human form, its severe wound healed. It held its arm and began running out of the restaurant.

"Kill them all!"

The husk screeched and lunged at the nearest security guard, and it was attempting to bite out his throat. Milton leaped upon the husk's back, using all his weight to pull it off. One of the security guards simply ran away, while the others stared in shock as Milton struggled with the shriveled corpse.

Suddenly, its head, arms, and legs twisted backward to face Milton, making bone-crunching sounds as it did so. This took the hunter by surprise, and he staggered back. Just then, Shelly, Lewis, Hemingway, and Darla burst into the room as Milton managed to hurl the husk off of himself. It landed on a surprised Hemingway, who fell flat on his back. The Walum Olum fell open and landed next to him. Hemingway pulled out his guns, but the creature pinned him by the wrists before he could take the shot.

"Ah, shit! Shit-shit-shit!" Hem complained.

Lewis heard the voices from the book. His eyes began to glow green as he repeated the ancient words. Milton was lunging for the beast, but he was too late. The creature was about to rip out Hemingway's throat when its head suddenly burst into an explosion of rotting flesh and bone.

"Ow! I think you deafened me!" complained the hunter.

"Lewis, how did you do that?" asked Shelly, astonished.

"I just read the words," said Lewis, shrugging. "I don't even know what I said."

"Oh, great!" said Hem sarcastically as he picked up the ancient book. "Then I guess I should be glad you didn't send us to the 5th level of Hell! You touch this book again; I'll put several bullets in you!"

"He did save you, cuz," pointed out Shelly.

"Was that it? Was that P.E.?" asked a hopeful Lewis.

"No," explained Shelly. "That's just one of the husks he leaves behind when it doesn't quite kill you."

"ACPD," said Darla, holding up her badge. "These are...deputies. We're handling this."

Milton picked up the old sleeve blade.

"Thanks for the assist, cuz," said Milton. "Let's put P.E. away."

"We need the rest of the cousins, Milton," Hemingway said, trying to reason with him. "Oh, my God. **I'm** the reasonable one in this situation. This is bad."

"He's on a rampage, Hem. C'mon!" insisted Milton, giving chase.

"A rampage? That doesn't sound good," said Lewis, increasingly worried and following Shelly and Milton.

"When a devil this powerful knows it's going to be caught and killed, it tries to kill as many people as it can before we take it down," explained Shelly.

Hemingway trailed after his cousin and looked back at Darla.

"Baby doll?" he asked.

"Yeah, I got it," acknowledged Darla pulling out her cellphone. "I'll evacuate the casino."

"It's a level 25 plus. Empty the city and call all the cousins! This is a family reunion-level event!"

Chapter 10

The Eater ran through a crowd that had lined up to see the Strip Off. P.E. was bleeding and angry when it reached two colossal security guards at the entrance to the dressing rooms. They immediately pegged him as trouble, and the fiend was in too much of a hurry to be subtle.

"Get out of my way," it demanded.

"You'd better step the Hell back, son," said the sassier of the two.

The sassy security guard put a hand on P.E. He twisted the guard's arm around until it snapped. The guard screamed in pain, but P.E. shoved him against a nearby pillar, cutting the scream short and knocking him unconscious.

The second guard pulled out his mace and radioed for backup. Unfortunately for him, the mace did nothing.

"Mmm, spicy," quipped the fiend.

He grabbed the second guard by his jacket lapels and pushed him up against the wall. The incubus didn't normally eat male souls, but he was injured, and the soul would nourish and heal him.

"No! Let me go! Sweet Jesus!" squealed the terrified guard.

Fortunately for the guard, he happened to be a devout Christian. As the Eater's face began to open again, the silver cross that hung around the guard's neck tumbled out of his shirt and landed on the exposed skin of the fiend. It burned him like it had been made of molten steel. The creature howled in pain, threw the guard aside, and ran down the nearest hall to nurse his wound. The guard kissed his crucifix and began mumbling prayers as he backed away.

The cousins arrived several minutes later, and by this time, the place was swarming with casino security, two EMT's and some cops. The cops were about to close down the Strip Off to help evacuate the casino, but the incident had slowed them down. Hem pulled Milton back around the corner and stopped Shelly and Lewis from blundering into the cops.

"Goddammit! He's too far ahead of us now!" Hem spat.

"No, he's not," insisted Milton, looking at Lewis. "Use your sight, Lewis. Find him."

"I gotta touch the book," said Lewis.

"No! No friggin' way!" insisted Hem, stepping back.

"I don't know what I'm doing," admitted Lewis. "Your mother was helping me. I could hear her when I had the book."

"Just let him touch the book, Hem," pleaded Shelly.

"That could be my mother, that could be the book pretending to be her, that could be a demon--- "

"Devil!" corrected Lewis, shocked at being betrayed by that wordplay. "I can't believe you just said it that way!"

"Hem," vowed Milton. "I am not letting this quarry get away."

Milton handed his cousin the sword and then straightened out his jacket. He emerged from behind the pillar to the officers and inhaled deeply from the nose as if preparing himself for battle.

"Sir? Can I help you?" one of the cops asked, putting his hand on his gun.

"Oh, my God! He's gonna karate these cops, right?" said Lewis in anticipation.

"Cops don't actually fight each other that way," explained Hem.

Opening his wallet, Milton flashed his badge.

"Hey, guys. I'm on the job over at Abe's Hat. Milton Galloway," he said, introducing himself.

The tension immediately evaporated from the room.

"Oh, hey, I'm Brooks; this is Denison, McCafferty, and Smith," introduced the officer. "They're evacuating the casino; we could use your assist."

"Would love to help, but I was actually looking for a perp. Handsome guy, slashed in the arm?" Milton said routinely.

"Yeah! That's the guy that attacked us!" said the sassy guard from a stretcher.

"You must've just missed him," concluded Brooks. "Going to be impossible to find him while evacuating the casino. But we got plenty of cars outside. We'll get 'em."

"Yeah, well," said Milton, trying to steer the conversation back to where he wanted. "I'm pretty sure this guy has got a thing for some of the strippers. If you could just let us into the Strip Off."

"Sorry," apologized Brooks. "I gotta shut it down in a few minutes. There's only so much I can do for ya."

At the same time, the Eater had gone outside. It contemplated leaving to roam the country on his usual murder spree, but the fiend really wanted to end things with Milton. Not kill him, per se, but break his spirit. He couldn't possibly put this in the win column if it left now. It needed more mayhem and death. It spotted some of the strippers catching a cigarette outside a fire exit. He rushed for it as it was closing and grabbed the door.

Inside was the mother lode. The dressing room for the Strip Off was full of gorgeous 20-somethings, prime beauties that were toned and ready to bare it all for cash and prizes.

"Ladies!" he announced to the room while locking the door. "If I could have your attention!"

The flesh from his face pulled back, and the strippers screamed in terror.

A few halls away, Milton was doing a dance of words, trying to get a fellow officer to do the favor he needed without quite knowing why.

"Thing is, Brooks," said Milton, pulling him aside and gesturing to his cousins. "My cousin over there? The girl, Shelly, she was assaulted, and we were just looking to teach this perp a lesson...kinda old school?"

"C'mon, man, seriously?"

"We'll take him out of the casino and back in the woods. He won't be anywhere on your turf if he...suffers an accident. I swear," assured Milton. "Very discreet."

"You gotta **swear**, and they all gotta buy tickets for our chili cook-off fundraiser," insisted Brooks. "Plus, I gotta perp of my own I'd like to bring out to Abe's Hat. Maybe do a tap dance on his head?"

"Well, then I gotta ask if you're cool with bringing your patrol cars to our car wash in two weeks?"

"Only if you buy at least three cakes at our bake sale and one has to be from my wife."

"Okay, but I need a Right Fielder for my softball team."

"As long as you agree to be our backup for the bowling team."

"Uh..."

"Oh and--- "

Milton shook his hand, cutting him off.

"Look, send me an email. I don't remember half the stuff we just promised each other. If you forget, just call my captain."

"You got it!" agreed Brooks. "You owe me one."

Milton stopped in midstride, then thought better than to restart the conversation and continued on. The group walked inside the hall where the Strip Off was being held. It was a cavernous chamber, darkly lit with three stages decorated with poles and mirrors.

"Well, that was anti-climatic," said Lewis.

"I would've kicked their asses, Lewis," assured Hem, a bit sad. "It's just the P.C. culture of today."

"Ladies and gentlemen," said the announcer. "I've just been informed that the Strip Off will have to be postponed for tonight."

The audience immediately started booing but then applauding as one of the strippers strutted out on a dark stage.

"Our apologies," continued the announcer. "But we'll have to continue this later. Wait--- Is one of the girls on stage? Let's turn up the house lights so people can see."

The audience started to applaud and whoop, hoping to at least get a taste of the Strip Off before being forced to leave. But when the lights came up, the stripper was clearly a dried husk. It screeched at the audience. The unnatural abomination was enough to unnerve the horny crowd, and the room fell into a panic.

"He's backstage," concluded Milton. "Save the audience, Hem."

Milton charged through the crowd and headed for backstage.

"Milton! Wait!" Shelly called after him.

Hem strapped the goggles back on.

"Nobody get in front of me," he announced, whipping out two pistols.

Hem rushed the stage, with Shelly and Lewis trailing behind him. The stripper husk dropped down and grabbed an obese man in the audience who was still trying to get out of his row. The man screamed and tried to pull away. Hem got to the end of the row and whistled at the creature. When it turned toward him, he blew its head off in one clean shot.

"Nice shot, cuz!" added Shelly.

"That was too easy," concluded Hem, lifting the goggles.

Just then, the remaining strippers, all of them husks, came pouring out of the backstage like a horde of hungry beasts.

"See?" added Hem strapping the goggles back on.

"Gimme the book! I can cast something!" insisted Lewis.

"No!" insisted Hem. "Intern, give him the starter weapon."

Shelly pulled a super soaker from her backpack and handed it to Lewis.

"What the Hell is this?!"

"Super Soaker full of holy water, so you don't hurt civilians," explained Shelly, pulling out her crossbow and cranking.

Hemingway was picking off the undead strippers one by one. He was steadily taking them down, but as always, he got cocky. With the sensibility of an 80's action hero, he gradually began caring more about his fantastic one-liners than actually landing a shot.

"This is for lapdances under two minutes! And this is for those hot wing buffets no one even eats! And this is for no sex in the champagne room!" said Hemingway, listing his various strip club complaints.

Hemingway got to the stage as one of the dried stripper husks leaped for the pole. With her droopy tasseled breasts flopping in the breeze, she spun around and kicked Hem in the face hard enough to knock him on his back. The creature picked up Hem as she spun around the pole and lifted him up and down, banging him against the stage as she slid up and down the pole.

"Ow! Shit! Lil' help!"

Shelly fired her crossbow, nailing one of the creatures to a nearby wall. Lewis pumped the Super Soaker, and the holy water burned the ghoulish strippers. Shelly scrambled to reload the crossbow.

"Hurry up! Hurry up!" panicked Lewis. "The water's only slowing them down!"

Backstage, Milton had been jumped by two stripper husks but made short work of them with his sword. P.E. sucked the last of the life out of the last stripper and set loose her dried, screaming corpse. The martial artist cut it in half and then lunged at P.E.

"So many delicious souls, buu-uuddy!" taunted the fiend. "You got a new girlfriend these days, Milton?"

The devil picked up a rack of stripper clothes and broke off a metal bar to block Milton's sword. They battled back and forth for a few swings. Milton was a practiced swordsman, but the creature was just fast, strong and vicious. Getting in close, he slashed the beast across the chest, and the fiend threw the martial artist into a make-up station and a mirror.

"You're fun to fight now," P.E. admitted, noticing black blood running down his hand. "Wait a minute."

Milton had managed to slice off P.E.'s pinky finger in the melee. It lay on the floor, trying to inch its way back to its owner.

"Ah, shit!" muttered the devil.

The creature rushed forward to recover it, but Milton was ready. P.E. blocked the sword, but Milton kicked him down a short flight of stairs to the fire exit. Pulling out a bottle of holy water, he uncorked it with his teeth and poured the entire bottle onto the finger. It burned him like acid, and the devil howled in pain at the bottom of the stairwell.

Out front, the remaining horde of undead strippers rushed Hemingway. Lewis and Shelly were, too, being overrun. One of the creatures jumped on Lewis's back, and he spun around, firing the Super Soaker, trying to hit her.

"Goddammit, I have to do everything!" complained Hemingway.

Pulling out a squirt bottle from his jacket, Hemingway sprayed barbecue grease on the pole. Unable to maintain her grip on the pole, Hem and stripper ghoul immediately feel to the stage. While the creature was distracted, he hurled a pocket full of marbles from his front jacket pocket onto the stage. The other stripper creatures, still wearing impossibly tall platform shoes and heels, fell in random directions, unable to keep their footing.

Hemingway tried to reach one of his guns, but the stripper husk held him against the pole. Unsheathing his silver hunting knife, he hacked off one arm, then the other, and pulled himself free.

Shelly had reloaded the crossbow and tried to eye up a shot against the one holding Lewis.

"Shelly! Wait!" he begged.

She bashed the creature across the face with the crossbow rather than firing it. It fell off Lewis, and she pinned it to the ground with a crossbow bolt. Suddenly, Lewis and Shelly heard gunshots. Hemingway had recovered one of his guns and shot five of the creatures in rapid succession. As two more charged forward, he let the empty clip from his automatic fall to the ground as he pulled out another. At the same time, he jumped off the stage just as the ghouls reached him. The monsters attempted to stop at the edge of the stage, but their footwear had no grip, so they slid off on either side of him. By this time, Hemingway had reloaded and quickly dispatched both of them before they could lay a hand on him.

At the same time, the Pussy Eater had already run outside the casino and was heading for the boardwalk. Black blood was pouring out of the spot where its finger had been severed. Milton was running close behind him. The fiend waved his arm, causing a casino jitney to fall over in front of the hunter. Milton ran around it and continued to pursue him up the ramp to the boardwalk towards the crowds of tourists out for a late-night stroll.

Hemingway and the others had finished off the remaining stripper ghouls, then followed Milton's and P.E.'s path backstage. Along the way, Hem and Shelly had reloaded while Lewis kept demanding a better weapon.

On the boardwalk, P.E. was running, but Milton was determined to catch up. He took out a silver Chinese star and hurled it at the fiend. It struck it on the leg, causing it to stumble. Milton charged, but the creature waved its arm, causing the boardwalk boards to turn into a wall between him and Milton.

Before Milton could get around to the other side of the makeshift wall, the creature rushed into a small enclave of seats that had an overhang, which was used for live music events outside. It stood in the middle, then circled the spot allowing its wound to bleed a circle, closed its eyes, folded its hands over its chest, and disappeared inside the ring. Hemingway and the cousins arrived just as Milton climbed over the wall.

"There he is!" shouted Hemingway, blasting a nearby air conditioning unit mounted on a nearby building holding carnival games.

"Hem! Take those stupid goggles off!" snapped Milton. "He's here. He's close."

"Look around," Hem instructed Shelly and Lewis. "But don't stray out of eyesight."

"What am I looking for?" asked Lewis.

"Something weird," explained Shelly.

The duo drifted toward the enclave.

"Shelly, I'm sorry," apologized Lewis.

"Now is not the time, Lewis," she insisted.

"No, it is. I screwed up. I screw up everything," Lewis admitted. "But I'm not sorry I met you. You're awesome, and you deserved better than me blowing up your spot."

"Lewis, I cannot process this now!" said Shelly. "There may be something between us, but right now--- "

"There's something," finished Lewis.

"Lewis!"

"No, I mean, there's black stuff in a circle right here," said Lewis. "Is that for like a spell?"

"Hem!" called Shelly. "There's a weird circle on the ground!"

Lewis's vision gave him a glimpse of the Pussy Eater underneath the boardwalk. His tentacles were growing through the supports and boards like veins.

"Run! Everyone run!" screamed Lewis. "Back away! Back away!"

Lewis and Shelly ran out of the enclave as Hem and Milton ran toward it. The cousins changed directions the moment boards started erupting out of the enclave. They twisted and began to form a giant, 50' tall demonic entity. As the boards and infrastructure of the boardwalk were pulled toward the spot where the fiend had started his spell, they twisted in a circle causing the boardwalk to collapse under the cousins and pull them toward the center and the creature. The depression caused them to slide closer to the monster, and no one could seem to get their footing to climb out.

"Nuts to this!" blurted Hemingway.

And with that, he let go, pulled out his guns, and fired as he slid down towards the hole that opened up in the boardwalk.

"Hem! Wait!" shouted Milton.

As Hemingway reached the hole, the Walum Olum fell out of his jacket and stopped at the hole's edge. Hemingway fell in. As he

90

fell, he could see pieces of rebar left behind by the fiend in a small field of spikes to impale him. Quickly accessing the space, Hemingway straightened his arms and legs and landed himself sideways between the bars.

"Ha-ha! Dick!" he shouted.

The bars suddenly wrapped themselves around him, and he was held fast.

"Oh, shit," he said, surprised by the turn of events.
Lewis noticed the book at the edge of the pit. The boards were disappearing to build the demonic creature, and it could fall at any second.

"Save him," Aunt Christie's voice rang in his head. "Save my, boy, and I will reward you! I swear it!"

Lewis gave Shelly a kiss.

"What the Hell are you doing?!" shouted Shelly.

"Something stupid!" said Lewis, sliding down toward the book.

He grabbed the book and stopped just short of the hole. Pulling it back, the gambler started reading. Arcane energies surrounded Lewis and emanated from his eyes. He and the book began to float, a new force of energy fighting the wave of devil magic. A wave of power came off of Lewis and the book. It threw Milton and Shelly out of the hole and bent the rebar back so that Hem could escape. Lewis' spell seemed to culminate, and a blast of energy came down from the clouds. It split the giant demonic entity in half, trapping it. On the opposite side of the energy was a Hellish landscape of fire, brimstone, and flying devils.

Milton and Shelly found Hem standing on the beach, pointlessly firing at the creature. The wind was kicking up, and there was electricity in the air.

"That's not going to work, cuz!" shouted Shelly.

"Don't ever say that about my guns, intern," chastised Hem. "Guns always solve problems!"

"Jesus! Lewis just opened a portal to Hell!" shouted Milton. "I don't think Aunt Christie could even do that!"

"I need a bigger gun," insisted Hemingway.

"We gotta get to its heart!" insisted Milton.

"I'll just go borrow a step ladder!" said Hem in frustration.

Looking up at the monstrous boardwalk creature, the cousins could see P.E. under its "skin" directing its movements. It was trying to pull out of the portal to Hell but could only swing its arms in anger.

"I can see him!" said Shelly. "He's up there! I'll take a shot!"

"You gotta better chance of him impaling himself than you making that shot!" said Hem. "No offense."

"That was incredibly offensive and demeaning!" assured Shelly.

"Just let me take the shot," said Hem, trying to pull the crossbow out of her hand.

"No," said Milton. "I got this."

Near the boardwalk, the Strip Off had set up a giant billboard and had strapped it down with metal cables. They were pulled very taught, and at the angle, they were aimed right at P.E. should they snap.

"Take the shot, cuz!" shouted Milton, gesturing to the support.

"You want to commit suicide--- Why you have to drag me into it?" snapped Hem. "Ooo, I am on it when we get into a fight."

"Just do it!"

"This is crazy! Even for me!"

"Do it!" insisted Milton.

"You're badass, cuz!" said Hemingway, shielding his eyes. "Stay back, intern."

Hemingway took a couple of shots and eventually shot the metal cable as Milton held on. With the tension suddenly released, he shot up like a rocket toward the trapped devil spawn. Milton's sword became the tip of the missile, and he pierced through the chest and blasted out the other side. Several hundred feet away, Milton used his martial arts to twist and turn and slow his descent. He landed feet-first in front of a boardwalk soft-serve establishment. A little kid who saw the commotion came out of a t-shirt place and ran toward Milton. Milton gestured for him to stop, and a second later, his sword came down, sticking itself deep into the boardwalk with the Pussy Eater's heart kabobbed on it.

"Whoa," said the kid, happy to avoid being impaled.

Milton stood, picked up the sword, and kicked the heart off the blade and into a nearby trashcan. He sheathed the sword on his back scabbard and looked back at the creature. P.E. was screaming in agony. The thousands of souls it had taken over millennia now poured out of him and toward a bright light in the heavens. As Milton watched, he spotted the ghostly form of Denise emerge from the chaos. She looked back at him and then floated into the light toward her final reward. Milton wept.

The mystic energies that had lifted Lewis and the Walum Olum now faded on the beach. He collapsed to his knees on the sand, and the book bounced shut. Shelly climbed down from the boardwalk while Hemingway strode over from the rebar.

"Lewis! You did it!" Shelly beamed, giving him a hug.

Hemingway aimed his pistol at Lewis.

"Get away from him, intern," he said grimly.

"Hey!" objected Lewis. "I just saved your life. How about a little gratitude, piney?"

"Gratitude?!" snapped Hem, outraged. "You colossal fucking idiot! Do you have any idea what you've done?! Look!"

Hem gestured with his gun toward the screaming fiend. His demonic boardwalk monster was raining down pieces on the beach.

"Yeah, I did what you do," said Lewis, incredulous. "I killed a devil."

"Moron! Shelly, tell idiot-boy where devils go when we kill them here!"

"They go back to Hell," explained Shelly. "I don't --- "

"He's standing halfway in Hell and halfway in our world! He's got nowhere to go!"

As P.E. disintegrated, the fiend let out one last, ear-piercing screech heard for miles in every direction. Its boardwalk body collapsed, and its actual body turned to dust and blew away.

"You stupid, stupid shit!" ranted Hemingway. "These things already hate my family enough! You actually destroyed one of them! One of the big ones! They're gonna rain down shit on us like nothing before! More people are gonna die! All because of you! All because you wouldn't leave the books alone!"

"No, Hem!" Shelly begged, placing herself between her cousin and Lewis. "You don't understand. Lewis is important to me."

"Get away from him, Shelly!"

"I'm not going to let you hurt him!"

"We have to kill 'em before it's too late!"

"No! I won't let you! You'll have to kill me!"

"Goddammit," said Hem, lowering his weapon. "There's going to be a reckoning, Lewis. There's a price when using the books!"

"So what?" said Lewis defiantly. "The shit I've done. I'm already going to Hell. At this point, what else they gonna do to me? Huh?!"

Without warning, Milton ran across the sand and tackled Shelly out of the way. A few seconds later, a new portal opened up, and demonic hands and arms came out and grabbed Lewis. It pulled him, screaming back through the portal.

"Hey, what the fuuuuuuucccckkk!" he screamed.

"No!" screamed Shelly pushing Milton aside and getting to her feet.

Shelly took a silver chain with a hook out of the backpack with an X. More silver chains unfurled as she moved, pouring out of the bag.

"Hold this, cuz," she ordered Hemingway, taking charge.

Hemingway took a few steps toward Shelly to stop her, but she threw the blunt end of the hook into his knee, causing him to stumble on the beach.

"Ow! No! Shelly!"

"Wait, Shelly!" called Milton reaching for her. "You never tested the backpack!"

With the chain unfurling out of her backpack, Shelly jumped into the portal after Lewis.

"I am so angry and proud of her right now," commented Hemingway. "By the way, I have so many complimentary things to say about your badass devil slaying today, but they'll have to wait."

"The portal's still open," noted Milton. "How do we save her?"

"The chain's her only hope, cuz," assured Hemingway.

"Y-y-you ever seen anything like this? Your mother maybe?" asked Milton hopefully.

Hemingway secured the hook around a remaining boardwalk support and rubbed his knee painfully.

"Relax, I know what to do," assured Hemingway. "My great Uncle Chaucey fought some devils near a portal. Let me go get the truck. You guard this chain. Don't let it go anywhere, cuz."

"You got it," assured Milton.

Hemingway patted him on the back in rapid succession and quickly limped for the truck. Milton watched the chain and noted that it moved around inside the portal. As it did so, it tore part of the fabric of reality, making the portal slightly bigger. He tried stepping on it to slow the process, but the result made the chain go straight down, tearing an even bigger rip and making the hole more prominent and making the chain move even more.

"Uh, oh," muttered Milton to himself.

Chapter 11

In Hell, Shelly tumbled down to the end of the chain and found herself on a fiery landscape of rock, brimstone, lava, and hellfire. She remembered her cousins and a few aunts and uncles telling her what to do if she got sucked down to Hell. The number one rule was that the longer you stayed in Hell, the worse it would get for you. It was imperative she find Lewis and exit as quickly as possible. The devils wouldn't kill Lewis, quite the opposite. The fiends would relish a live human to torture for his entire natural lifespan. They had all eternity to torment his soul, but his body and mind were a novelty to be relished. As was hers.

"Lewis?"

Almost immediately, she found Lewis cowering by a rock formation.

"Shelly! Oh, God! Help me, please!"

"Lewis! Come this way!"

Almost immediately, as Lewis started rushing over to her, she realized the entire setup was too easy. She pulled out a smaller super soaker and squirted Lewis. He immediately burned, revealing a Level 6 Shifter. It screamed, blinded momentarily, and Shelly took the opportunity to pin the creature's foot to the ground with a crossbow bolt.

"Where?!" she demanded.

Back on the beach, Hem skidded to a halt on the sand and then backed his truck so that it was against the boardwalk support. He jumped out of the vehicle. Milton noticed he was wearing a bandolier of loaded magazines for his pistols. Hemingway took the chain and hooked it to a winch in the bed of his truck. He flipped the switch to wrap the chain around a couple of loops, taking up the slack good and tight. By doing that, the chain in the portal moved even more rapidly, and by now, the hole was the size of a bus at the edge of the water. Milton looked into the portal and could see the Hellish landscape and winged devils flying in the distance. One of the fiends looked in the direction of the portal. Hemingway was rapidly arming himself.

"Um, Hem, what exactly happened to great Uncle Chauncey?"

"Oh, he killed a record number of devils and died horribly," revealed Hemingway matter-of-factly while loading a shotgun. "I got some spare swords for you, but you might want to strap some guns to yourself too."

"I feel like you're burying the lead, Hem," prodded Milton. "What's going to happen?"

"Well, the longer Shelly is in Hell tied to this chain, the bigger that portal's going to get, and it's just a matter of time before--
- "

The winged devil flew out of the portal with a screech. Hemingway blasted it to pieces with the shotgun while Milton reeled.

"That's going to start happening a lot," explained Hemingway. "Would you mind?"

Milton cut the heart out of the devil. Its chest cavity blown open by Hem's shotgun blast, so his blade quickly cut through the black flesh. He cut off its head with a flourish. The creature disintegrated and reconstituted inside the portal without its head. It flew into the nearest outcropping of rocks and then plummeted out of sight. Hemingway looked just about ready to fight anything; he had strapped so many guns to himself.

Milton looked out onto the Hellish landscape beyond the portal, which was getting bigger and bigger. A massive horned devil with a multi-bladed sword pointed at the portal and began yelling at other devils to charge at it. Milton stared for a moment in shock and then punched Hem a few times to alert him.

"Jesus, Hem," said Milton. "What are we going to do?"

96

"Defend the beachhead, cuz," said Hemingway, cocking his shotgun. "And I'm going to get some trophies."

"Trophies?"

"Yeah," said Hemingway picturing it. "They're gonna dedicate a whole **wall** in the Lodge to us!"

"We're gonna die, you idiot!"

Hemingway shrugged.

"No need to be negative, cuz," he said. "It's going to be a fabulous wall."

Back in Hell, Shelly had duct-taped the Shifter to the end of her crossbow. She knew that if the Shifter could take Lewis's form, it must've bitten him.

"I'm not sure where he is!" begged the creature. "You're hurting me!"

Shelly took out her silver pocket knife with a four-inch blade; she slashed at the devil, severing one of its fingers.

"Ow! Why?!" it squealed.

"For every thirty--- No, ten seconds I don't see Lewis, you lose a finger," she threatened.

"But I beg of you! Please!"

Shelly cut off another finger. The creature finally dropped its helpless personae.

"You are not so easily swayed," the fiend noted, smiling sinisterly. "I will take you."

"Make it quick," she insisted. "And I don't have any problem taking your junk as a trophy."

The creature led her through Hell. The path turned on a cliff face. Below, several devils were building what looked like a massive complex. Part of it resembled Abe's Hat High School, various pieces of Abe's Hat, and what looked like the Galloway Farm.

"What is that?" Shelly demanded.

"We build personal Hells for everyone," said the creature routinely.

"Who is that one for?"

The fiend smirked knowingly.

"You already **know** who it's for," said the creature. "Did you think your cousin would live forever? When you see him, tell him we're **waiting** for him!"

"Where's Lewis?!" Shelly demanded, raising the knife.

Pointing with one of his remaining fingers, Shelly looked up. It was an old apartment door that had been built in the rock. Shelly opened it. The smell of cigarettes, feet, and Lysol was almost overwhelming. Inside was Lewis's dad's old row home. Lewis stood in the center with his head down, being chastised by a monstrous incarnation of his dad.

"You're a failure! I wasted my life raising you?!" ranted the old man.

"Dad! Please! I don't belong here!" begged Lewis.

"You're pathetic! You belong here more than I do! You lie! Cheat! Steal!"

"Lewis!" called Shelly.

The Shifter pulled at the duct tape, tearing it just enough to turn away from the bolt. Shelly fired, but the bolt lodged into the old T.V. in the corner. For a second, Lewis turned away from his dad. Shelly and the Shifter struggled and fell behind a divider in the apartment.

"Look at me when I'm talking to you!" insisted Lewis's dad. "You show me no respect!"

Lewis went right back into his personal Hell.

"I do respect you, dad! Please! You're always riding my ass!" insisted Lewis tearing up. "I can't be like you!"

"You are like me! You're a loser! A loser that's going to die alone in a filthy rowhome in South Philly!"

"No!" insisted Lewis, slowly consumed by his own despair.

"Do you feel it?" whispered the Shifter struggling with Shelly. "Do you feel the despair in the air? You soon will know its taste! For eternity!"

Back on the beach, Hemingway started playing the Beastie Boys' "Sabotage" on a continuous loop for the fight. He shot devil after devil in the face with his shotgun while Milton attempted to cut out their hearts before they could recover.

"Woo! This is my new favorite video game! Defend Atlantic City!" proclaimed Hemingway. "GTA ain't got nuthin' on me!"

One of the flying devils got past the cousins and attacked a group of onlookers at the fringe of the chaos.

"Hem!" Milton shouted, calling it to his attention.

Hemingway was stepping on the neck of a devil he had kneecapped. He eyed the shot up and fired. The flying fiend dropped like a stone.

"Okay, new plan!" shouted Hemingway.

The hunter blew off the arms and feet of the struggling devil, leaving it screaming and bleeding on the beach.

"We don't kill 'em, just maim them to the max!" proclaimed Hem. "Every devil gets a handicapped space!"

This was more in Milton's wheelhouse. The swordsman drew a second sword and started chopping off the arms of the devils. He followed through with kneeling and cutting them off at the knees. The fiends fell to the sand, screaming and flailing their bleeding stumps helpless. The black blood of the devils was spraying in all directions, darkening the beach and water.

Hemingway tried to fire his shotgun but was out of ammo. A Level 7 Marrow Sucker, standing about 8' tall and covered with scales, batted the gun out of his hand and knocked Hemingway off his feet. The hunter quickly recovered and kneecapped the devil with a pistol. It landed face-first at him, and he promptly shot it in both eyes. It squealed even louder.

"Ya see?!" shouted Hemingway over the chaos. "This is why I needed that fifty-caliber machine gun mounted to the back of the truck!"

"Can we talk about that later, Hem?!" said Milton, dodging and a particularly quick devil with a pitchfork.

"If those guys at Fort Dix hadn't been such pansies, I'd be kicking ass at 500 rounds per minute!" insisted Hemingway.

"Cuz! Those were soldiers!"

"Yeah! And I paid for that .50 cal! What the Hell good are my taxes if I can't arm myself with a weapon of mass destruction when I need it?!"

In Hell, Shelly struggled with the Shifter, who tore at the backpack.

"What are you wearing?!" it demanded.

It grabbed the chain and burned its hand.

"Ah! You bitch!"

Lewis was still having a moment with his dad. He couldn't seem to shake the despair.

"Lewis!" called Shelly. "You have to face your worst fears here! You have to own them, or they'll own you!"

"You're a disappointment, Lewis!" continued his father. "A worthless piece of shit! A whore, just like your mother! You'd do anything for a buck!"

"That's not true!" Lewis argued weakly.

In the background, Lewis began to make out the sounds of Shelly screaming, but he couldn't hear the words.

"You know it's true! You know you're selfish and worthless! You don't care about anyone but yourself!"

"No," insisted Lewis. "I care about Shelly."

Shelly was trying to reach for the knife she had dropped, but the Shifter turned into another version of her.

"This'll be nice," whispered the Shifter. "His love to torture him for an eternity!"

Hemingway and Milton were now knee-deep in paraplegic Hellspawn. Hem had a rip in his hunter's jacket, and Milton was bleeding from a small cut on his forehead. The martial artist had resorted to decapitating the devils, and their heads and bodies were stumbling down the beach and into the surf. Hemingway got bum-rushed by a group of devils that he just managed to dispatch with his pistols. Deciding that he'd never be able to reload in time for the next wave, he tore off a pocket on his jacket, revealing a silver hand grenade. He pulled the pin and tossed it.

"Fire in the hole, cuz!" shouted Hem, diving away.

Milton heard the call but wasn't sure which way he should leap. The hand grenade exploded, taking out several devils as they crossed the threshold. They befell the same fate at P.E. and were sent to oblivion. Another devil that had made it through was about to stab Milton with a sword, but the shrapnel hit him from behind. He expired, collapsing on Milton, who then realized what had happened.

"You bought a hand grenade?" asked Milton.

"Okay, the Fort Dix guys weren't **total** buzzkills," admitted Hemingway. "But I only brought the one."

One of the winged devils landed on the back of the truck and attempted to figure out how to disconnect the winch. It poked at it curiously until Hemingway pumped a clip of bullets through his heart.

100

"Hem! They're figuring it out!" noted Milton, cutting down three devils that vaguely resembled samurais.

"We just have to give Shelly enough time!" insisted Hem.

The humungous devil that had ordered the Hell troops through now reached the portal. He was ten feet tall with massive horns and held a nasty-looking sword with multiple blades. His skin was yellow-gray, and his face looked like a mean-looking cat. He batted away some of the other devils in his path with his sword while charging Hemingway.

"No!" insisted the giant devil. "This one is **mine**!"

"Oh, fuck **me**," muttered the hunter aloud.

"I will!" assured the fiend. "I will rape your battered corpse until it splits in half!"

The fiend charged. Hemingway fired a barrage of bullets, but the creature held its sword up to its face to protect its face and head. The hunter changed gears and tried to kneecap the charging fiend, but his knees and lower shins were armored. The bullets bounced right off. Hemingway was forced to jump out of the way as the devil brought its massive sword down at him.

"Milton! You may have to hold the fort for a minute!" shouted the hunter, running for cover under the remaining boardwalk.

"Hem!" Milton shouted but almost immediately realized a new problem.

Two of the devils were standing on the back of Hemingway's truck, trying to figure out how to dislodge the silver chain without touching it. Milton did a flip over some devils, landed on the pickup, and cut the two fiends down, sending body parts flying. When he turned around, he realized he was now making a last stand on the back of the truck with dozens of devils clamoring all over the beach.

"You will pay!" shouted Milton, inaccurately quoting the Shogun Assassin movie as he slashed and hacked at anything that got near him. "In rivers of blood!"

Chapter 12

In Hell, Lewis was finally confronting his own demons in devil form.

"You can't do anything for yourself! Physically a grown man, but you act like a child!" insisted the monstrous form of his father. "You expect me to take pride in you?! I'm ashamed of you! I've always been ashamed!"

"So what?!" said Lewis defiantly. "I didn't make you live in this shithole and smoke yourself to death! You did that!"

"You're pathetic!"

"No, **you're** pathetic! I got my own life, and it may not be perfect, but it's mine! I don't need your approval!"

"You don't have it!"

"I don't care! I'm my own man, dad!"

As the Shifter struggled with Shelly, it became aware that Lewis was beginning to break the hold of his despair. It was just enough of a distraction for Shelly to gain the upper hand. She couldn't reach the knife, but she looped the silver chain around its neck. It immediately started burning the creature. Unable to pull the chain or keep it from burning into its skin, it returned to its proper form and started squealing in pain. Lewis finally shook himself free of the hold the monster dad had on him and turned around.

"Shelly?!"

"Lewis! Watch out! It's not your real dad!"

The monster dad rose out of its seat, becoming more and more demonic. Lewis staggered back, unsure of what to do. Shelly burned the Shifter's head clean off its neck. Grabbing the head, she leaped upon Lewis' back and handed it to him.

"Hold this. First, kill," she explained.

"Aw, man!" said Lewis in disgust.

Shelly flicked the switch on the backpack, and the winch inside it started to retract. She and Lewis were pulled backward out of Lewis's personal Hell as the monster dad roared. They burst through the apartment door in the rock and were back outside with the fire and brimstone.

"Whatever you do, don't let go of me!" instructed Shelly.

"I'll never let **you** go," said Lewis suavely.

"Not really the time, Lewis," noted Shelly.

"It's never the time," said Lewis, annoyed. "When is the time?!"

Under the boardwalk, Hemingway was using every trick at his disposal to dodge and duck the massive devil stalking him.

"I will break your bones!" it ranted, smashing a boardwalk support. "I will suck the marrow from them until there is nothing left!"

"Dude! What did I do to you?" said Hemingway, sensing this was more personal than normal. "If you're gonna kill me, why be a dick about it?"

Hemming way peeked out from behind a concrete support and fired a few bullets. The creature brought down its sword as Hemingway took cover again. A cement block, hidden in the sand, held the sword fast. Hemingway stepped out again and sprayed the creature with his mister of holy water. It staggered back, the water burning its face.

"Eat that, ya prick!" proclaimed the hunter.

Hem followed up with a barrage of bullets, shooting four of the creature's fingers as it shielded its face. It howled in pain as Hem laughed, but his laugh was cut short when the devil backhanded him. Hemingway flew through the air and into a crowd of the devils charging Milton. The creatures swarmed him.

"Hem!" screamed Milton, trying to hack his way off the truck.

A few seconds later, Hemingway stood up and threw the devils off him with a silver collapsible baton, which was also electrified. In his other hand was a silver Bowie knife. His hunter jacket was torn to shreds, and he had bloody cuts on his arms, chest, and beer belly.

"This is starting to piss me off!" shouted the hunter.

The giant devil now charged through the crowd of devils like an angry bull. It lowered its horns, impaled several of his own troops trying to get to Hemingway, and then knocked the hunter for another loop. Hemingway lost both his weapons and landed on the sand some distance away hard.

On the other side of the portal, Shelly and Lewis were drawn into the logjam of devils. As the chain wound into the backpack, it no longer bounced around, making the portal bigger. The portal was now naturally closing. Several of the creatures attempted to grab the silver chain but only succeeded in burning themselves. They kicked and scratched at Shelly and Lewis. Shelly reached into her backpack and pulled out a device that resembled a water balloon with a tiny radio. It beeped, and she tossed it in the air just above them. It burst, spraying holy water in the immediate area, causing the devils to stop attacking them for the moment, but the chain wasn't retracting anymore.

"Lewis! We're stuck!"

Through the chaos at the portal, Lewis spotted a glimpse of Milton on the back of the truck. He concentrated on the hillbilly samurai.

"Milton!" said Lewis in his mind. "Pull us out, cuz! Pull us out!"

Milton could make out the voice in his head.

"Lewis? Where are you?"

"The other side of the portal! Pull us out! Now!"

Milton got the message, and after kicking a few devils out of his way, he kicked the switch to the winch. Unfortunately, there were too many devils on him. When he kicked it, they immediately pushed it back.

On the beach nearby, the giant devil ripped the impaled devils off his horns. Black blood poured down his face, burning his eyes and blinding him a moment. Hemingway was standing right in front of him when he got his eyes clear, popping him in the eyes with the sleeve gun. It howled in pain and swung wildly. Kicking it in its throat, the fiend gagged, and he threw the little gun down its gullet. It started to choke.

A group of devils came running to assist its general, but Hemingway threw what looked like a handful of silver marbles at them. They burst on impact, releasing clouds of silver dust, causing the creatures to choke and collapse.

Hemingway took out his key chain, extended the silver chain, and attempted to choke the large fiend to death. Unfortunately, the creature's neck was just too large. Hemingway couldn't quite get the chain around him. It burned its neck, and the creature reached behind, grabbed Hemingway, and slammed him onto the beach as hard as he could. The hunter bounced and moaned in pain.

"What the Hell, man?" asked the hunter, coughing up a little blood this time. "What's your problem?"

The devil began to recover, took a few steps, and picked up its sword.

"Hemingway," it began sinisterly. "I am the brother of the one you defeated!"

"You gotta be a **lot** more specific," said the hunter trying to get to his feet.

"Todd sends his regards!"

In that split second, Hemingway realized, much to his horror, that he had been fighting one of Todd's brothers. The resemblance was now so obvious, he was mentally chastising himself for not seeing it immediately. But as the creature raised its sword with two hands, there was a shotgun blast. The blade came down with two devil hands still wrapped around the hilt. Black blood was pouring out of the wrist stumps and out of the arm stumps of Todd's brother. The devil squealed in agony, unable to stop the bleeding from either arm. It tried to press the stumps together, but it was just short by a few jagged inches. Hemming way turned from the direction of the shot. Along a section of boardwalk that hadn't collapsed were the rest of the Galloway hunters led by Byron.

"Fire at will, cousins!" shouted Byron. "It's trophy time!"

A barrage of gunfire now mowed down the devils on the beach, and with their general writhing in agony, many lost their will to fight and tried to retreat into the portal. It was closing and was now completely jammed with devils. Milton now had enough of the devils off of him that he was able to start the winch again. On the other side of the portal, Shelly and Lewis were being pulled through the panicked Hellspawn.

"Hey, old man!" called Byron to Hemingway.

Hemingway bristled. He was limping, and his left hand was holding his side.

"Well, that's just great!" snapped Hemmingway. "Now I have to share all these kills!"

Byron tossed him a hand cannon. A Desert Eagle.

"Oh, this is nice," said Hemingway.

Hemingway walked up behind the wounded devil and shot it through the back.

"I'd tell you to give Todd a message," began the hunter. "But you're gonna see him very soon."

Hemingway blasted the fiend's neck, all but severing the head from its body, then kicked it off the rest of the way. Its horns stuck into one of the wooden boardwalk supports that had fallen over. Sticking the gun into his belt, he limped over to the devil's sword, pulled off the hands, and limped back with it. He stabbed the bloated, headless body in the chest. The head screamed in pain, and a fountain of black blood sprayed everywhere.

"Holy shit, how much blood do you **have**?" said the incredulous hunter.

On the truck, the winch was struggling against the tangle of devils trying to get back into Hell. It pulled off its base and started bouncing toward the closing portal. Milton leaped over a horde of devils and stabbed his swords in the sand ahead of the winch base. The blades were now cutting along the beach as they were being pulled toward the portal, but Milton managed to hand crank the winch to bring Shelly and Lewis closer.

"Hem! Help!" called Milton.

Hemingway emerged from the devil's open torso carrying its large, bloated heart. He was covered in black ichor. Throwing the heart down onto the sand, he rushed to grab the chain ahead of the winch.

"Forget the winch! Just pull! Byron! Cousins! Get over here!" called Hem.

The Galloway hunters had turned the tide, and they rushed to the chain. After a few seconds of pulling, the portal began to finally close. It made that weird engine noise, sucking in all the devil bodies on the beach.

"It's closing!" shouted Byron. "Everyone pull! Pull now!"

At the last second, Lewis and Shelly tumbled out of the portal as it closed behind them. Lewis rolled off of Shelly, exhausted from the experience. His clothes were singed and tattered.

"Oh, my God," gasped Lewis. "Thank you! Thank you so much!"

"Don't thank me yet!" said Hemingway, getting to his feet. "I saved one bullet for you, Lewis!"

Shelly threw herself on top of Lewis while the other hunters in the Lodge tried to reason with Hemingway.

"Cuz, c'mon," said Byron.

"He opened a book, Byron! This whole thing is his fault!" snapped Hemingway.

"**You** brought him into the Lodge, ya turd!" pointed out Eliot.

"Shut the Hell up, Eliot!" snapped Hem. "You gave him the book!"

"He was just trying to help!" insisted Shelly.

The cousins started to bicker, but it was Lee that shouted down the mob.

"Wait-wait-wait!" shouted Lee. "He's a cousin!"

"What? Bullshit!" insisted Hem.

"I haven't finished the test, but the markers are definitely there. He's **family**, Hem," said Lee. "Science doesn't lie."

"This is nuts!" snapped the hunter.

"You were going to shoot him in cold blood on the beach in Atlantic City," pointed out Milton. "How nuts is that?"

"I'm sorry, cuz," insisted Lewis. "I'm sorry."

"No! No!" said Hem.

"He's a cousin; he can say it," assured Byron.

"Oh, my God! I can't **believe** you guys!" ranted Hem, handing the Desert Eagle to Byron. "Sweet piece, by the way. But still, this is nuts."

There was an awkward silence. In the distance, there were police sirens. They were getting closer.

"What do we do now?" asked Lewis, unsure of what to do. "What happens? We go back to the Lodge?"

"No," sighed Milton. "This is where we all go to jail."

"Everyone stashed their cigarettes, right?" asked Eliot hopefully. "Cause a pack ain't gonna last me."

The police sirens were actually FBI sirens. Federal Agents now swarmed the beach in tactical gear screaming for the hunters to drop their weapons. They quickly complied, and the entire Galloway clan was rounded up, handcuffed, and thrown into paddy wagons.

Later, as the Galloway clan was being hauled off in chains, Lewis tried to get the lay of the land.

"You guys got a cousin in the FBI, right?" he asked hopefully. "W-we're not going to jail, right? You guys did this before, you said."

"Normally, we don't destroy half of the Atlantic City Boardwalk and like fifty strippers in the process," said Hemingway, annoyed. "Last time we did anything close to this big, I went to jail for six years."

"**Six** years?!"

"Yeah, and nobody died that time. That was just property damage. We're going away for life, **cuz**," explained Hem bitterly. "Hey, but don't sweat it. One day in the prison yard, and I'm going to shiv the **shit** out of you, so you won't be there that long."

"Hem! C'mon, man! I said I was sorry! Why are you so pissed at me?!"

"Because I don't like you, Lewis! You don't listen! You open books! My mother--- Y-y-you open books! I told you not to open the books!"

"Wait a minute," realized Lewis. "You're **jealous** of me."

"Why would I be jealous of **you**?"

"Because your mother reached out to me instead of you. You're actually jealous and fighting over your mother's attention! What are you? Ten?"

"I'm gonna kill you, Lewis! I swear to God, the second I get loose! You're dead!" growled Hemingway, pulling against the chains.

"Hemingway," chided Byron. "For God's sake, he's family. You know you're not gonna kill him. You're fine, Lewis. Trust me."

Lewis was unsure. He looked back at Hemingway, who just smiled and shook his head slowly.

Eventually, the truck stopped. The back door opened, and spotlights aimed directly into the vehicle made it impossible to see outside. Lewis heard the sounds of gates and prison guards. The Galloways were being dragged out of the truck one by one very roughly. Lewis could hear them getting beaten outside.

"No!" cried Lewis when it was his turn. "Please! I'll cooperate! I'll testify! I-I-I-I'll do whatever you want!"

They dragged him outside, and Lewis found himself in a gravel parking lot. The spotlights went out. They were actually mounted to a pickup truck parked outside the Hunting Lodge. Cousin Joyce was standing with the other cousins playing the sound effects on an old boom box while Darla was uncuffing the cousins.

"I'll do whatever you want!" mocked Hemingway in a high-pitched voice.

The other cousins burst out in laughter. Lewis looked around, and he spotted Shelly standing nearby. Some of the FBI agents were picking up the handcuffs and getting prepared to leave.

"Sorry," she said sheepishly. "They love this prank."

"You're an asshole, Hem!" snapped Lewis.

"Serves you right, though," commented Byron. "Not smart to touch the books unless you know what you're doing."

"**Never** touch the books, Byron," corrected Hem.

"You can do it once or twice if you **have** to," he insisted.

"Don't start this argument again," said Joyce. "He did just save your ass, Hemingway."

"I know he did, and let me just say to all of you," Hemingway announced diplomatically. "I am so proud of my former intern here."

Hemingway gave Byron a manly hug and slapped him on the back for good measure.

"Anytime, old man," assured Byron.

"And Shelly, my current intern, is an intern no more! Right, Shel?"

Shelly held the severed head of the Shifter, and a cheer rang out amongst the hunters.

"Aw, man," the Shifter muttered to itself.

One of the FBI agents shook hands with the cousins and reached Milton.

"Fitz, you're not staying?" asked Milton.

"After what you guys just did to Atlantic City? My boss is still wrapping his brain around how we're supposed to spin this thing, cuz," he said, mildly depressed. "You guys just dropped enough paperwork in my lap to last six months."

"Aw, c'mon, Fitz," said Hemingway. "At least stay for a drink and a burger."

"Not even rib tips are gonna cover this," assured Fitz.

"Hey, say what you want about Lodge, but **never** doubt the power of rib tips!"

"You had a cousin in the FBI?!" snapped Lewis.

"We have **six** cousins in the FBI," Milton informed him. "Two in the NSA and one in the CIA."

"Why do you think Milton's a cop? And Darla?" said, Hem. "It's the only way we can hide this."

"Uh, remind me why you didn't make it as a cop?" said Darla sardonically.

"Punched the instructor on my first day in the Academy, but in my defense, I really wanted to do it. So…"

"I think it's time we got cleaned up and had a celebration!" suggested Milton. "What do you say, cousins?"

A second cheer of agreement rang out. The cousins all began to disperse, and Hemingway helped Lewis to his feet.

"There's a separate apartment in the barn," explained Hemingway. "If you want to crash there until you can get yourself together, you're welcomed to it."

"Thanks," Lewis said, touched. "You really are treating me like family."

"Well, I'm obligated, but we gotta work on some things."

"So…Are we cool?"

"Yeah, we're cool. I sounded mad, but we were just hazing you. You're the new guy. Besides, I don't have time. I just want to see if I can score with the ex tonight," said Hemingway, trying to clean up his tattered clothes. "Meet you later. You gotta free beer coming your way."

Lewis exhaled, exhausted and relieved. A shower was just what he needed. Shelly was still showing off her kill to the other cousins.

"Shelly, I'll meet you over at the farm," said Lewis.

"Okay," she acknowledged.

Chapter 13

Lewis walked across Abe's Hat and back to the Galloway Farm. As he reached the edge of the property, his foot sank into a hole. He leaned on a nearby tree to catch his balance, which promptly collapsed. Fortunately, Lewis managed to roll away.

"Jesus! What the Hell!" he exclaimed.

Lewis climbed out from under the smaller branches just as Shelly ran up.

"What happened?"

"I don't know! I stepped in this hole, and then this tree collapsed---"

As Lewis told the story, he happened to glance across the street. Standing in the bushes, watching, was Hemingway. He pointed to his eyes with two fingers and then back to Lewis.

"Oh, my God! He's there!"

"Who's there?"

Hemingway stepped into the bushes and was gone.

"Hemingway! He did this!" insisted Lewis. "He really does want to kill me!"

"Lewis, you're being paranoid," assured Shelly. "You honestly think my cousin sabotaged a tree on his own property on the off chance you would stumble into it and get crushed? When would he even have the time to do this?"

"You know how he is! He's crazy! Y-you can't leave me alone!" insisted Lewis.

"Actually," smiled Shelly. "Being alone with you is exactly what I had in mind."

"We got time?"

"For a quickie."

Lewis decided that sex with Shelly was worth the risk. Who knows? Maybe he was being paranoid. The couple had a quick, intense sex session in the shower. It was probably time to tell the cousins about their relationships anyway. There's was no way Hem or Milton could object to it now. And it wasn't like they were real cousins. Odds are they were removed by several generations anyway.

"Okay, I guess it's time to tell them," agreed Lewis. "Although I could really use a drink before that."

"I think Hem has a bottle of whiskey in his kitchen by the fridge," Shelly informed him.

She kissed him and went to finish getting dressed. Lewis, who had his shirt off, walked upstairs and peered into the kitchen. He didn't want to get caught partially undressed before the explanation. Seeing that the coast was clear, he reached up to open the cabinet near the fridge.

Unfortunately, the knife rack that hung across the sink was caught on the edge of the cabinet. When Lewis opened the cabinet, it pulled the end of the rack off, causing the knives to slide off suddenly and rain down near where Lewis was standing. He narrowly averted, getting stabbed in several places below the waist.

"Jesus Christ!" he exclaimed. "What the Hell?"

When Lewis looked up, he caught a glimpse of Hemingway standing outside and watching him through the kitchen window. He was so startled by his appearance he reeled and fell backward on a kitchen table.

"Holy shit! Oh, my God!"

Shelly came rushing into the kitchen and helped Lewis to his feet.

"What's going on? What happened?" she asked.

Lewis looked, but Hemingway was gone.

"Your cousin is what happened!" insisted Lewis. "He's trying to kill me! Look at what he did with the knives! He caused them to fall!"

"Lewis," said Shelly trying to calm him down. "I know my cousin is a bit nuts, and we've all been through a lot in the past couple of days---"

"You can't leave me alone!"

"Lewis, we're family! He can't kill you now!"

"Why does everyone keep saying it like that?! Like he could kill me if we weren't distantly related?!" panicked Lewis. "What's to stop him from killing me in an accident and blaming the accident?!"

"Look, Hem is a lot of things," admitted Shelly. "Stubborn, impulsive, arrogant, kinda misogynist--- But he's not a **psychopath**. He was tested."

"That last sentence is the least comforting part!" insisted Lewis. "Will you please just not leave me alone until we make our announcement, please?"

"Okay, okay," Shelly relented. "Get your drink and come downstairs."

Lewis hesitated. Shelly rolled her eyes and opened the cabinet, and there was the whiskey bottle as promised. She grabbed a glass and handed it to him.

"You really do need this drink," she said, handing it to him.

Shelly headed back downstairs, and Lewis immediately trailed after her. He stayed near her side until they were headed back to the hunting lodge. Lewis looked in various directions as they walked, convinced Hemingway was now lurking in every shadow.

"Will you calm down?" insisted Shelly. "You are really killing the vibe."

"I'm not killing it!" Lewis insisted. "He's--- He's hunting me!"

"Who's hunting you?" asked Hemingway.

Suddenly, Hemingway was standing behind Lewis and Shelly outside the Lodge. Darla was under his arm. Both had beers in their hand and looked a bit unsteady.

"You! You're hunting me!" accused Lewis.

"I am such an amazing hunter that I didn't know I was hunting you," slurred Hemingway. "How did I do…that?"

"He is **drunk**, Lewis. There's no way he's trying to kill you."

"The important thing is," belched Hemingway. "Is Darla drunk. Are you drunk enough to have sex with me yet?"

"Mmmm," said Darla thinking about it while finishing a bottle. "Two more beers."

"To the cooler!"

Hemingway and Darla staggered away to get more beers.

"See?" said Shelly, turning to go inside the Lodge.

As soon as Shelly turned away, Hemingway dumped the rest of his beer out and looked Lewis straight in the eye, sober, mouthing the words, "I'm not drunk."

"Goddammit," muttered Lewis to himself in frustration. "Goddammit!"

The party got pretty crowded and pretty loud. Far more members of the Galloway clan packed the Lodge than did during the barbecue. Shelly's first kill devil head was mounted and hung. Todd's brother was also mounted, and Hemingway repositioned the heads so that they would be forced to kiss.

"Broth-er," moaned the new head.

"You…are…an idiot," growled Todd.

At one of the tables in the lodge, Milton chatted up Joyce Whitaker. But he wasn't immediately looking to have sex with her. Something about the evening's events had changed him.

"Hey," she greeted as he sat down. "I was waiting for you to get back."

Joyce punctuated the statement by rubbing her foot along Milton's leg. He laughed but then composed himself.

"Listen, Joyce," he said. "I've been through a lot in the past few days. Reliving some of my past, putting some ghosts to rest. Quite literally. I don't think I can do this, okay? I'm just not ready mentally, ya know?"

"Oh, I'm sorry, Milton," she said apologetically. "It's okay. I might get back with my husband anyway."

"Oh," said Milton, a little taken aback. "Great. That's great."

"And here he is," Joyce noted.

As Milton stood to get up, Ronald Whitaker walked into his space.

"What the Hell are you doing with my wife, Milton?" he demanded.

Milton could smell the beer on his breath. He had picked the wrong time to talk to Joyce.

"We didn't do anything," assured Milton. "Not this time."

"Not **this** time?" he said, disgusted.

Whitaker punched Milton in the face, knocking him to the floor. Some of the other cousins intervened to break up the fight. Milton did not retaliate. Part of him thought he deserved a wake-up call.

Lewis went up to get some food and lost Shelly in the crowd. Relatives talked and clamored everywhere, and Lewis didn't really know anyone. Across the room, he spied Hemingway staring at him. Putting down his plate, he started to make his way out to the back bar of the Lodge. Despite all the supposed security, the secret passage had to be open to accommodate the rest of the family.

"Shelly? Shelly, are you in here?" he asked the room.

Blundering through the crowd, he found himself near the bookcase. It had been covered up with a sheet.

"You look guilty, Lewis," said a voice.

It was Cousin Eliot. He was a little drunk and kind of surly.

"Look, man, you gotta help me," begged Lewis. "Hemingway has lost it, okay? He's not just mad about the books---"

"No, **I'm** mad about the books," said Eliot. "You got me in a lot of trouble with the family."

Eliot staggered to his feet and almost lost his balance. Instinctually, Lewis reached out to help him. Eliot lost his balance and ended up pulling him into a restroom. When they got inside, Eliot suddenly stood straight up and smiled.

114

"I'm not drunk," he said.

Lewis turned around to rush out of the bathroom, but Hemingway had already run in behind him and was locking the door.

"That's the problem with people who don't know pineys," said Hemingway. "They underestimate us. They think we're just a bunch of drunken hillbillies. Right Lewis?"

"Listen," said Lewis, very worried. "I didn't reach out to your mother; she reached out to me? Okay?"

"Oh, my God," muttered Eliot. "You are saying **all** the wrong things to him."

Hemingway grabbed Lewis by the collar and pushed him into a stall.

"You can't kill me! We're related!"

"People have accidents!" insisted Hem. "Ninety percent of the accidents happen right in the bathroom!"

"In the home," corrected Lewis.

"I don't know where you live!" snapped Hemingway.

"Hey! Heeey!" said Shelly, banging on the bathroom door.

"Shelly! I'm in here! Help me!"

Hemming way made a face and unlocked the door. He and Eliot went back to pretending to be drunk.

"Hem, will you leave him alone!" snapped Shelly.

"Who?" Hem said fake drunk.

"I saw you walk in here, Hem," said Shelly superiorly. "I know you're not drunk. Stop messing with Lewis."

"What do you care, intern?" said Hem, immediately correcting himself. "Sorry. Cuz."

"Well, you might as well know," began Shelly.

Milton suddenly rushed into the bathroom. He still had a bloody nose from his fight.

"What the Hell happened to you?" asked Eliot.

"Nothing, never mind," he dismissed. "Cousins, you need to see this."

"We're busy," assured Hem.

Milton grabbed him by the shoulder and dragged him out of the restroom.

"What? What?" demanded Hem.

The group went back outside in the cacophony of relatives. Lee had a piece of paper and was explaining something to

Hemingway, Eliot, and Milton, but Shelly and Lewis couldn't hear over the noise. Lee handed the paper to Milton and rushed back to the bar.

"We got some interesting news," said Milton over the noise.

"We do too," said Shelly, putting her hand on top of Lewis' hand and smiling at him.

"Lee finished the test," explained Milton.

"Yeah, we know," said Lewis, incredulous. "He told us."

"Right, but he narrowed it down completely," explained Milton. "You're an actual cousin. Like **a close** cousin."

"H-h-h-how close?" stammered Shelly.

"You're my second cousin, cuz!" said Hemingway squealed excitedly.

The hunter suddenly grabbed Lewis in a bear hug and lifted him off the ground. Milton patted him on the back, and Lewis looked a bit stunned. Milton let Eliot examine the test results.

"Holy shit," he muttered.

"This means you're first cousins with me and Shelly," explained Milton.

"**First** cousins?" said Lewis, shocked. "You mean like---"

At the same time, Lewis brushed his hands against one of the old timbers that held the lodge's roof in place. He got the vision again. A group of colonial hunters looked like Hemingway, Shelly, Milton, and a fourth guy who looked exactly like him. The vision disappeared, and he was back in the present.

"Yeah, like you're practically brother and sister!" laughed Hemingway. "I am so embarrassed we tried to kill you now!"

"I knew it!" snapped Lewis. "The tree! The knives!"

"Yeah, I also gotta go undo a bunch of other stuff. I am **so** stupid sometimes," said Hemingway, embarrassed. "But hey, it could be worse."

"How could it **possibly** be any worse?" asked Shelly. "You tried to kill my--- Him! Cousin...Lewis."

"Well, Milton told me he got the vibe you two **liked** each other or something," laughed Hem.

"Sorry, Lewis," apologized Milton. "I get a little protective of Shelly."

116

"Oh, sure!" agreed Lewis a little too much. "That would be weird."

"Yeah, first cousins is like Game of Thrones level shit!" laughed Hemingway.

"Oh, my God! Can you imagine?" laughed Milton.

"Mutant inbred children!" laughed Eliot.

"Hey, let's all have a drink," suggested Milton. "Or several. Now we have more to celebrate!"

"Again, I can't tell you how sorry I am," assured Hemingway. "Now that you're a real cousin, you're welcome to move in with me and Shelly. It'll be great! We can play cards!"

Hem rushed out of the Lodge to disarm whatever other booby traps he had set. Milton and Eliot went to the bar to get shots for everyone. Lewis and Shelly sat at a nearby table in stunned silence for a moment.

"I think, um, I'm gonna need another shower," Shelly said, trying to remain as neutral as possible.

"Yeah, me too," agreed Lewis. "By myself, in a different...shower."

Lewis looked down and realized they were holding hands again. They broke the grip and wiped their hands off uncomfortably. They realized now that they had a secret and that their romance could never happen. Lewis could hear the faint sound of someone laughing. He realized it was coming from the grave of Aunt Christie.

The witch had had the final laugh after all.

Made in the USA
Middletown, DE
20 February 2024

49413997R00071